# At That Very Moment

# At That Very Moment

**Mridula Sinha**

**Ocean Books Pvt. Ltd.**

**ISO 9001:2008 Publishers**

*Published by*
**Ocean Books (P) Ltd.**
4/19 Asaf Ali Road,
New Delhi-110 002 (INDIA)
e-mail: info@oceanbooks.in

ISBN 978-81-8430-387-2
**AT THAT VERY MOMENT**
*Stories by* Mridula Sinha

*Translated by*
Dr. R.K. Sinha

*Edition*
First, 2016

*Price*
₹ 250.00 (Rupees Two Hundred Fifty only)



*Printed at*
R-Tech Offset Printers, Delhi

*Dedicated to*

*My Eeya (Mother)*

# Introduction

Dr. Mridula Sinha is an eminent writer of Hindi literature. She has written more than 40 books on various subjects related to women and social problems. She has depicted the women characters, their strengths and weaknesses. This is a collection of her popular short stories. In 'My Shisha Phua (Aunt)' the main character can be found in any village of India. In 'Unveiling of the Statue' Prabhat's mother-in-law is a great lady. She has inspired her for higher things in life. In the 'Tiffin Box', she depicts the disintegration of the big joint family as it is happening in India today. The 'Borrowed Light' draws the attention of Indian youth to come back to India to solve its problems. Mother of Prakash is a typical village woman, firm on staying in the ancestors house of the village. 'On the marriage of a child', a Muslim woman narrates the story of her husband's love and care for her. In the story of 'Not Disposable', Gauri's Mother-in-law tells stories associated with different items brought for disposal after the floods but ultimately the vender is sent back. In 'A mother of Countless Children', the writer depicts the life of a nurse, her devotion to the children born under her care. The nurse didn't have time to marry but at her death, hundreds of people born under her care gather for her last rites. In Kaki's Pilgrimage, the writer depicts the character of a village woman who is bold and determined. She takes women to different places of pilgrimage and ultimately she dies in a Kumbh Mela. Her last rites are performed by a girl. This is a message to the Indian masses, the girl child can perform last rites. 'When Chaos Prevails' is the only short story available depicting the atrocities during the emergency years (1975 to 1977). Smt. Mridula Sinha's character depictions is unique. In the 'Pickle Earthen Pot', she depicts character of her philosopher mother. In the story of 'The Light Festival of a Lamp', she depicts the story of a village boy serving in a urban situation as a servant. He is not surprised by big things and occasions in the town. He always remembers his mother living in the village.

The stories are full of scenes related to life in the village and towns of modern India. The problem of working women is dealt with in the story 'Delaying Divorce'. Writer's stories by and large depict the picture of transition of India from village to Urban living and problem arising there from.

I thank Shri Anshuman Abhishek, OSD of Smt. Mridula Sinha, Hon'ble Governor of Goa for preparing the translated copies of the stories.

**—Dr. R.K. Sinha**
Ex-Union MoS
Retd. University Professor of English
(B.U., Muzaffarpur)
New Delhi

# Contents

# 1

# My Sisha Phua (Aunt)

Radha's husband's death spread like a fire in the village and atmosphere was remorseful. Everybody ran towards her house. There was a heavy crowd in her courtyard and verandah. A huge crowd gathered and everyone was silent. Radha's heart breaking cries were doubled by her mother and an other women. At that moment, a boy came running and said "Sisha aunt has come." This made everybody silent. It was an offence to cry before Sisha Aunt. Everybody moved towards the door to see Sisha Phua. A shrill of loud voice ran through the crowd and said "where is Radha, where is her mother" and Sisha Phua ran inside to search for them. Both of them were lying on their faces. Her voice rang, "why you are lying in the darkness?" She brought them outside, made them wash their hands and mouth. Her personality was such. She didn't like to stop and was never tired. She was as transparent as glass. In times of difficulty, she would certainly come through the village and she would inculcate courage in others. She was living idol of courage and patience. Radha saw her face in the glass and stopped crying. She felt a new strength inside her. Everybody in the village knew her as yeoman ship, as sister of nine brothers. Her father had two sons and two daughters. Her uncles had sons real brothers, there were only two sisters nobody known that why Sisha aunt never accepted her sister's identity. Since childhood, she would bestow affection on his younger brothers. She would move right through the village with elder's brother's son in lap. Her aunts were happy with her. "My elder uncle liked my serving of food to him." "It used to lit hukkah(I) for my other younger uncle". "One of my uncles could not enjoy food without my presence." She would always tell about her relations with all the members in the family. I and my sisters, Naraynai, Vidya, Shanti, Usha, Geeta would seat round her. She would speak high of her own good luck and belittle our status. I was alone, not a dozen like you. You are Swarm of locusts (Tiddi) on the house of your brothers that is why you are not honoured properly. We used to tease her, "Aunt who cares for you now? All your father and uncle are dead, now it's our time, you are old and rejected". Aunt was against old culture and fashion, she would speak out, and "Don't you see my brothers are not at ease without me. They always invite me for big and small occasions in the family. You can ascertain it from my elder brother (writer's father)". She had so many instances for supporting her claim. Our collective, strength would not stand before her loud voice. In her absence,

Kaki used to tell us, the joint family, father, uncles and nine brothers, didn't live any stone un-turned during her marriage. They spent beyond their capacity to search for a rich family and handsome groom. The marriage party was the talk of the time for neighbouring villages. But within a year, a messenger came with a bad news of the death of her husband. This made her father, numb. Nobody took food in the house for many days; nobody had courage to go to her village to know the details. A great scholar of Ramayana, middle uncle had blessed her at the time of departure, "May your husband live long, till the Ganges and Yamuna flow". After some time, she came back to her parents place, this created a sensation in the village. Who has come? Nobody has gone to call her. Everybody was surprised to see red cover doli, from which a woman alighted. Her mother went to take her from the doli. For the last fifteen days everybody was sad and full of tears. But she was smiling while meeting everybody. How would others weep, since then nobody talked of her misfortune. Not even her mother, in her absence, one may weep as much one could. After her marriage, the family was divided into four parts, but for her, every house was her own. She would take food where ever she liked. There were no restrictions on her. In the village nobody in her presence wept on her misfortune. In fact, she was proud of her good luck. She would always describe affection of her nine brothers. The women of the village forgot that she was a married woman. Her youthful nimble and adolescent talk, the ornaments of her ears, neck and armrest were always there. Only forehead was without Vermillin. She never accepted widowhood and how can others have courage to impose widowhood on her. After some time when it was disclosed that she was in family ways, everybody prayed that, may God give her a son. But when she was blessed with a daughter, there was no trace of sadness on her face. After two years, she decided to go to her husband's house, she said Uncle; "I will take this girl to her grandfather's house". All the elders sitting on veranda were stunned by her sense of practicality. Her husband's people didn't impose any restrictions on her. She was free to go her father house whenever she liked. Her brother-in-law (devar) respected her. She was conscious of her duty to her relatives and conscious of her own rights. She got her share of land separated, her brother-in-law used to look after her land. Their own land might remain untilled, but the land of Sisha Phua was always looked after properly. Now her daughter was young enough to marry. Her in laws were worried; it was not easy to find a good groom for her. She would sit in the middle of the yard and would describe the list of presents to be made to her daughter and son-in-law. Everybody at in-laws place was on his toes to discharge his/her duty. At the time of the daughter's departure to her husband's place, she hardly wept.

Now, she used to spend at least two months in pilgrimage. She used to take her neighbours to consult doctors in the town. For young men, she looked for their employment & talked to officers, if required. On the occasion of marriage she used to purchase everything from ornaments to sarees. All these were her daily routine.

Last time she came at the time of the marriage of her niece and she pervaded the whole atmosphere. She was consulted about every ritual. She showed the gifts, she had brought for Manju. She had brought flat rice, pulses and curd to help her brothers. Everybody at in-laws place was on his toes to discharge his/her duty. At the time of the daughter's departure to her husband's place, she hardly wept and then she would start, describing, how much grains came to her house in last five years, how much she sold, how much she spent on pilgrimage, how much she spent on the daughters of devar. She would describe the complete details. Somebody commented her brother in law doesn't respect her. She couldn't tolerate disrespect of her husband's side in the father's house and vice versa. "What are you saying", she would retort angrily. "You are not equal to a fifth of my devar." That day I suddenly changed the topic saying", Phua, you look tired." "No, I am not tired; I have returned from Pashupatinath and next month, I am going to Rameshwaram." She used to listen to everybody and tell her own story to them. Listening to her, people generally forget their own problems. Her presence was helpful in the marriage of someone's son or employment of others. In her presence, nobody had courage to weep, she herself never wept. She never asked any help from anybody; she only gave to others. To her brothers, nephew and nieces and neighbours. She gave them money, grain, clothes and above all, consolation and courage to fight. After marriage of Manju, she was ready to go to her home. Her bhabhi was weeping at the departure of her daughter, she scolded her. "Now stop weeping and arrange quickly for my departure, if you have some sweets, give it to me". I cut a joke to Phua, "you are greedy, Without taking sweets from bhabhi, you are not ready to go". Although there is nobody to take sweets to your house, I was sorry for my comments, she told me, "I don't take sweets. There are many children, if I go empty handed, they will ridicule my father's house. Many times, I purchase some sweets from the bus stand and distribute among the children". I asked Phua, "Does that land belongs to you? "Why not", she said, "As long as I am alive, I will not give it to anybody, "will you register the land to your daughter", she replied quickly, "No whatever I had to give her I have given her, I will register the land in the name of my devars. They have taken good care of me; I cannot be unjust to them. After death, what answer I will give to God". Suddenly she used to be very lively and said, "I am not going to die soon, I want to live, not die". The 70 year old woman was not ready to accept death. Surely her vibrant life was like drops of nectar for ordinary people.

Radha had relished that drop of nectar, she wiped her tears. Ultimately, Sisha Phua also had to face death.

Bhabhi told me how Sisha Phua was waiting for death, I did not believe, the family disintegrated in her life time. She gave up hope to live; only she could see and hear. All brothers and daughters were competing for the land to be registered in their name. She had lost her voice; her daughter prepared the land deed and aimed for her signature. She got angry, that made her daughter nervous. Her brother in laws (devars) did the same. For the first time, Phua pleaded to God of death, "Take me soon". The members of her family were now free to do whatever they liked. They were free to cry near her dead body and distribute her wealth and property amongst themselves.

□

## 2

# Unveiling of the Statute

On the main gate, a white stone statue was covered with a cloth. Before going to the podium, one has to unveil the statue by removing the clothes. I could remember the previous day's function of a book release. I thought, what is the difference between release of a book and unveiling of a statue? I got the answer from the inside, one is of paper and other is of stone, both are lifeless. But, the stone carved in a statue and the paper with letters become lively. That is why it is prohibited to touch them with foot. Papers written with letters and figures and stone carved in a statue. Both are the things to worship. Books and statues, both are dedicated to the people.

My mind was engaged in these thoughts and my legs reached the place of statue. I left my sandals and climbed the platform on which the statute was placed. Its height was five feet. Having unveiled the statue, my eyes concentrated on the eyes of the woman in a statue. Suddenly my eyes brimmed up, but I controlled myself. People were applauding, Prabathi and her relatives were happy, I got tears in my eyes. After taking my place on the dias, I started analysing the situation. It was the unveiling of the statue of Prabhati's mother-in-law. But I remembered my own Mother-in-law. The drops of tears were not so much for Sarashwati Devi, the mother-in-law of Prabhati as they were for my own mother-in-law, Banarasi Devi.

I got some thoughts for my speech, I did not know much about the domestic lady, Saraswati Devi. After her death, she was worshipped her by grateful children, what can be said about this? We need to talk and listen on these subjects. Children don't look after parents. After death, the rituals are hastily performed. Infact, we do not have time to shed tears for them. These types of lectures made the audience also weep. The house of Prabhati was in the vicinity. We stopped for some time there for tea and tasted some sweets. We were near Konark, it was nine o' clock at night and we started straight for Jaggarnath Puri. Since 1962, I have visited Jaggannath Puri many times. Every time, I used to hear new stories about the statues there. Pointing to the big ear of hanuman statue, the panda said, "Because of nearness to the sea waves, Bhawan Jaggannath appeared to be sad. After deliberation, it was decided that only Hanuman could manage of the sound of the sea. That is the way hanuman ji is in reclining position and his long ears face the sea. He stopped the sound of the sea. Now the sound is heard only after coming out of temple, not inside.

Similarly, we heard something new about Prasad, prepared there. Having seen the statue of Subhdra between Balram and Krishan, I was moved. In this material society, the colours of love between brother and sister have faded. I had darshan of the three statues at close quarters and I was happy. It was almost eleven at night when we reached the guesthouse and At 12, we went to the bed. On the next bed, Prabharti was lying, she said, "My mother-in-law was a great person, she always supported her daughter-in-law and not her sons".

She told me some more stories, I could not sleep. Before my eyes, the statue of Prabhati's Mother-in-law appeared. I sat on the bed and prepared myself for her stories. Prabhati was anxious to tell the story of her mother-in-law. She said, "After I cleared B.A., my husband and father-in-law were not ready to allow me to study law. But my mother-in-law was adamant. She said, "Prabhatri will be a lawyer". Everybody knew about her. She was true to her words. She helped me in studies and she would look after my daughter, I was a student mother. Once I purchased a doll for my daughter, when I went inside the room, I found the doll was not there, I was worried. I had imagined my daughter would play with the doll and this doll one day would come into the role of a mother. But where is the silent doll, I asked mother, "Have you seen the doll? "Yes it's here", she pointed towards my daughter sitting like a doll on her lap, I burst into laughter, "Not this but the toy doll I brought", I continued searching for the doll, she spoke very firmly, "My granddaughter will not play with dolls. Bring such toys, which will make her a doctor. In my village, many people died because there were no doctors. That very evening, I brought some medical equipment toys. It made her happy. Aishwarya used to play with dolls. I saw the dream in the eyes of my mother-in-law of Aishwarya becoming a doctor. She used to pose as a patient and Aishwarya would examine her as a doctor and prescribe medicine. One day Aishwarya was adamant, "I will be patient and you be a doctor". Her grandmother quickly lifted her from the bed and said, "Now my child will not be a patient, you have to be a doctor". It is five years since my mother-in-law had died, my daughter has passed the entrance examination for medical. I feel my mother-in-law is always with me. After listening about her mother-in-law, my interest grew more and I asked, "Did she ask for domestic work". Prabhati said, "Before going to husband house, I knew I had to prepare food. My mother had taught before my marriage, she had told me, "Your mother-in-law will teach you further." But my mother-in-law did not allow me to go to the kitchen. She always asked about my studies. One day at my insistence she allowed me to go to the kitchen. But in the evening she told me rice and pulses were half cooked. "Your vegetables were tasteless. I prepare better food than you", I was afraid, "Do not think much about it. I am used to prepare food since I was 8. Sometimes rice were uncooked and vegetable tasteless. I could not prepare chapatti properly, my mother-in-law used to' teach me. But now food prepared my me is appreciated. Even in darkness, I can prepare properly".

It was not worthy to become daughter-in-law of such a mother-in-law. She told me, "I have brought a graduate daughter-in-law. In the village there is no house with such a daughter-in-law. I know you have no training for cooking. You have been using pen and I ladle (kalchi). Don't try cooking any more, you have to study and become an officer or a lawyer". I could not assess whether my Mother in law was expressing her desire or she was commenting on my ignorance of cooking. After some time, situation was clear. She wanted to see me in a chair and at disposal of file, but for her the work of a lawyer was much more important. She told, "You are an MA now and you study law. There are many women in my village who do not have knowledge of law, nobody is there to fight for them". She made me to study law, "You will stay in Cuttack and practice law". She came to me to live with me at Cuttack. She used to look after my two daughters, Aishwaya and Prachurya. She was very happy to see me in black coat. She used to touch my heavy books, think something and smile. One day she told me, "I have spent whole of my life in cooking. Sometimes guest had tasty food and sometimes tasteless. But my constant effort and hard work brought a day when the food prepared used to finish within fifteen minutes. Then suddenly said," whatever literature people write on the paper, does not faint. Your children can read whatever you write. My work is good but yours is better. I was stunned to listen to her thoughts. I asked her, "where was your father-in-law, there is no mention of your father-in-law in the story of your mother-in-law". Prabhati said, "My father-in-law was living in the village, He was working in a post office. What was his role in your education? Did he agree with his wife about your study? Prabhati said, "In this matter, my mother-in-law was much clear. She used to take proper care of her husband and gave him respect. But she used to say, look! your father-in-law was alone. It was after the marriage that family was formed, I look after the children and he never consulted about his office work. So I thought why I should consult him in rearing my children. Whatever he decided, I supported, he didn't interfere in my work. On the second day of every month, he used to give his total salary to me. I used to look after the agriculture interest, used to sell grains. Never did your father in law ask me account of income from agriculture".

She used to listen to new ideas of the new age, at my house and in my office. Generally, cases of marital problem would come up. I would take these cases, she used to listen to these things. The moment I went inside, she would begin, "Prabhati, this kamla who came today was talking lies about her husband, I think, she is herself culprit, I think her husband is innocent". Mom I need to go court now, I have taken up the case of Kamla and you are pleading for her husband. If I listen to you, I will be confused in the court about the case. She would say, "But there should be justice". She came out and told me, "Prabhati, you don't take fees from Kamla". Her words kept me haunting in the court, perhaps I could not plead properly for Kamla and I lost the case. Even this defeat made me happy, many people congratulated me but I didn't respond to them. According to my profession, I should have won the case but the congratulations on defeat made me obtuse. My mother-in-law was against her son, when my second daughter was born. She didn't listen to her son. My husband wanted to have, third child. But my mother-in-law was adamant, "what are you talking, she had two daughters, why should she wait for a son. Prabhati is also a daughter but what is the difference, to give birth to a child is not an easy job. Women who go to court as a lawyer, how will she look after children? In the hospital, there was a big crowd": The lecture of my mother in law in favour of daughter was applauded. I underwent the operation at that very time four other operations were held.

By mother-in-law evolved as a leader. But she didn't like joining my politics, having watched my interest in politics she said, "Why you do this? Is the work of your lawyer not enough for you?" "But I will do both the work; there is no harm in it". No your law practice will stop; you will give more time to politics. She didn't like my decision of joining politics, but I didn't want to hurt her. She used to ask me that what benefit I would get from this. She was not enamoured of my post in political party but had a vision for red beacon car. She made a compromise. When she was bed ridden she said, "Prabhati even if you move in red beacon car, don't stop fighting the cases of poor women. What for their literacy, that is why I brought a graduate daughter-in-law", Prabhati looked towards me and said, "Was not my mother-in-law a great woman? Her eyes were brimming with tears. I said the statue in the evening was of stone. In the last four hours, you have unveiled a personality of late Satyawati Devi. She will always live in you. She will always be alive till your daughter and their children will live. Such unveiling inspires generations". She said, "You are correct; my mother-in-law lives in daughters". Aishwarya said, "My grand ma is my ideal. Kasturba Gandhi, Mahadevi Verma, Indira Gandhi were helped by many people; they were given opportunities. My grandmother is great and a large hearted even without getting an opportunity. Greater than educated women, I will fulfil her dream of being a doctor". You are correct; "Your mother-in-law will survive in your daughters. She will tell her children about the greatness of her grandma. Perhaps they will also say "She was a great lady".

It was almost morning: It took five hours in unveiling Satyawati Devi's personality. My hands folded at the realisation of it being morning, my words came out and I recited the morning mantras and name of Sita, Savitri, Ahalya, Tara, Mandodri. These were the five great daughters. They are born again and again, and this is their unveiling along with unveiling of Satyawati Devi. I was submerged in the second unveiling.

□

# 3
# Tiffin Box

Ram Niwas, famous house of the town went on increasing number of rooms. As the family increased, wealth also multiplied. Ram Niwas had tour sons. Out of four, his two sons had two sons each and the other two had one son each. All sons had one daughter each, it was a big family. With the increase in numbers, they had to increase the number of rooms. But they had one kitchen; it was big enough to accommodate about dozen for dinner at a time. Three to four women could serve them; about fifteen to sixteen persons could at a time be in the room. The head of the family had not distributed the duty of serving meals to the daughters-in-law. Some would peep into it and if two or three were there, they would engage in some other works. There was no lack of work in the house. The clothes of about three dozen people had to be washed, dried and ironed and then distributed to the irrespective rooms. The second daughter-in-law was expert at this. She used to examine all the pockets of male members before giving it for washing. Every day some money would be found in the pockets and sometimes big amount was also found. She used to return money to the persons. This household affair was like a company in which there were management experts. Santosh ji, eldest daughter-in-law of the house was CEO. She used to arrange tiffin boxes for children going to school and male members going to offices. Her husband used to sit in a cloth shop. Santosh ji would occupy the kitchen early at six in the morning. After all, preparing tiffin for fifteen children and five elders used to take time. She knew the taste of every one and used to fill the boxes accordingly. She would come out of the kitchen and go to bath and then visit temple within two hours. She would come to the kitchen again at eleven after breakfast by that time, lunch was ready and with great care, she used to prepare the tiffin boxes for the elders. If she was unwell or on visit to her mother-in-laws place or go to some pilgrimage, the tiffin boxes would return from the offices without use. This filling of boxes continued for 25 years. She had trained her daughter in laws also for the same. But gradually number of tiffin boxes went decreasing. Now grown up children didn't like to take tiffin boxes and she also gave up her insistance.

I frequently visited her house. I came to Delhi; sometimes I used to go to Lucknow. Five years back I went to Lucknow, one purpose was to visit Santosh Ji. I was attracted by large hearted woman in a big house. She never differentiated among the four brothers. Every child would confide to her about his/her taste. I liked to sit and talk to her. My family was a small one. Those leaders, who are set on bringing socialism should have first learned in the primary school of Santoshji instead of reading books.

When I went to Lucknow I visited her house, the house looked deserted. I asked, "Where the people of the house are? Santosh Ji eyes were numb, she spoke "My father used to tell a story about birds". Santosh Ji looked at me, she said, "I visit a temple daily having a orphanage, there I fill tiffin for two hours. My one granddaughter-in-law and her children live with me. We have little domestic works to perform; I asked where all the people have gone? "Times have changed, new generations children don't like to follow job of their forefathers. They went to foreign countries, last month I was in America and was sad as few family cook food in the house. They take meals outside and children get tiffin in their schools. I don't feel happy there". I said, "Their values are different, in our country grandmother are available for preparing tiffin but time is changing in India also as hotels are increasing in numbers and the kitchen are deserted.

I sat with her for a long time, told her, "You are lucky at least your one grand son and daughter-in-law is with you". In the meantime their grand children and teacher daughter in law returned home from school. She opened the tiffin box brought by them, the daughter-in-law replied, "Today there was a farewell in school, so we could not use this tiffin". For last several days they have been making some pretext for not opening the tiffin box. Santosh ji was now tired and she decided to stop filling tiffin boxes.

Three years passed, a month back I went to Lucknow again, saw a big lock hanging on the door of the big house. I had apprehensions, may be like ripe mangoes, she might have dropped any time. I have seen the house in many phases. In its youth, it was full of life and activities, I saw the last stage of the house five years back and now the scene of sannyasi stage was before me. Someone came and asked, "Whom you search for in this house? One grand mother lives alone, she has a door on the back side of the house. She lives in one room, no kitchen and no puja ghar. I come here to give her a tiffin box".

I went to the back door of the house and a door open, I peeped and found Santosh ji sitting with a tiffin box before her. She was happy to see me. After sometime she said, "I can't offer you tea as nobody is in the house. Grand son and daughter-in-law had gone to Delhi. She has arranged a person for bringing tiffin box for me". "I don't understand", "why you don't understand in many houses now, there is no cooking, in this town a new system of tiffin supply has begun. For me every morning and evening a tiffin box comes. I asked, "If you don't like the food, do you return the tiffin box", she was lost in the past and replied. "One weeps only when somebody is there to wipe the tears. Tiffin may be returned, if there is someone to take care of your taste". I kept musing over this psychological answer born of experience. I asked, "If you like to have food of your taste what do you do?" "A single person has no taste. I used to fill the tiffin according to the taste of others. This became my habit. One by one every body has gone, had my father been alive, he would say the last bird has also flown away and here the story ends. I was soaked in the words of her experience. Now it was evening, it was time for Santosh to open her tiffin box. I got up; I took leave of her as if departing for the last time.

□

# 4

# The Borrowed Light

Prakash had made a special request to me, "This time, don't bring pickles, homemade sweets made by my mother. Now I am not a student as I have joined a job and purchased a flat. You bring my mother here so that I can enjoy delicacies prepared by her". "Will you not marry, your mother will ask me. What answers will I give, tell me". Tell her "I will marry next year, I have just joined the job."

"Will be American girl or..." my mother will be happy with this news I will think about the girl later. First you bring her here, you go to my village, you will like my village. It is between Muzaffarpur and Sitamarhi". He was happy to describe the live map of his village as if he was standing on the land of his village. I had decided that after reaching India I will go first to his village. I will get a photo of Prakash's mother for passport and visa. I was eager to earn the merit by helping a mother to meet her son. This idea had overwhelmed me after ten years a mother will meet her son. When I boarded the plane I forgot that I was returning to India after five years. My mother would be waiting for me with same eagerness. At the airport, when I met my mother I felt, as if Prakash was meeting his mother. There was a difference at least I could hear the voice of my mother on telephone. Prakash is mother had no such chance. I told my mother about the message Prakash had given me. My mother said, "Yes first you go and see Prakash's mother". It will take time to get passport and visa for her. Ultimately, I reached the village of Prakash, the search of village was for me like journey of Columbus full of thrills. Thousand kilometres by plane and then bus, rickshaw, Tonga and bullock cart. Some people alighted from the same bus I was travelling; I asked them the way to village of Prakash. They requested me to sit in the bullock cart. One of them said that they knew that I was about to reach there from America. Somebody uttered, "If any American gift rides in a bus to village its clear that she would meet Prakash's mother." I was surprised to find them considering me American, my jeans and shirt was burdensome to me. "Yes I have come to see mother of Prakash and take her as her son has called her". "We will take you to the village, why didn't Prakash come? Why Prakash has not come?", "He had taken a new job". I managed narrow path to reach the village and at a dilapidated house someone pointed this as Prakash house where his mother lives. Some children ran into the house and with them an old woman appeared. Her left hand was on knees and right hand above her brow. She asked, "Where is my son?" She came to ask me, the children laughed. I got hold of her. She pressed me to her chest. She was speaking "My son, everybody thinks me a mad woman. They use to say you will not come, He will marry there and settle in America, but I believe he will come one day and build this house. I will get him married; my daughter-in-law will come". Somebody told me in my ears, she has gone crazy. She keeps speaking like this, she heard this and she shouted at them. "Have I gone mad, go away from here? Leave me alone with my son". I thought it's necessary to clarify the situation and said "I am not Prakash, I am Shivani". She took a long breath and sat down. After sometime she asked me to sit by her side. She took my face in her palm and asked. "You are not Prakash, who you are?" "I am friend of Prakash and have studied with him. He has sent me to see you". She kept silent for long time: Perhaps she was searching for words to ask about her son. She left and went inside the room. She brought sweet porridge for me in a pot. She said, "Take it, the cow has given milk today after two days. Perhaps she got the message of your coming." While I was taking porridge she kept staring at me. I said, "Prakash is very happy there. He has a good job, now he is ready for the marriage". She interrupted, "what do you do there and where are your parents?" I said, "I am studying in America and parents are in Delhi, both are teachers in a college". "How old are you? "24 years", "Do you know cooking? "A bit", "I will teach you how to cook". "I will return today, I have to stay for two months in India, I will come to take you". "Then why did you come to me, did you consider me a mad person?" Her words surprised me. I had to pretend, "No no, I have to come to stay with you". "I wanted to know whether you liked me or not. "I have been deprived of human touch and company, tired of talking to cow, goats and parrot. I keep talking, they don't answer my words. These parrot always talk of Prakash, I am just a scare-crow. The parrot spoke, Prakash, Prakash Prakash has come, Amma, Amma, your son has come". She said, "Look how mad is this. Prakash had brought this from the forest. He had taught it to call Amma. Now he is old like me, the bird of the forest had become my pet and my pet is in a foreign country". Her eyes were full of tears, "You seat close to me. Prakash would always wipe his wet hand in my apron". "Your son is a good boy, he always remembers you, he has sent me to take you to America". She kept mum; perhaps she was happy with the news of going to America. "Now it's evening, I must light the lamp. Darkness was spreading, I was afraid of spending the night with that woman. She brought the lamp before me and asks to bow down. I folded both my hands, controlling herself, she said, "My son was four years old, he used to wet his bed. His aunt did a black magic, she kept burning lamp over his head and muttered the mantra, "You wet your bed, sleep in the house and piss outside" from next night he stopped wetting his bed. He was a healthy child but a naughty one. He was given a lantern by his uncle who used to say my nephew will be a great officer. He will join the military, "Where are his uncle and aunt", "One in Calcutta and other in Banaras". My mother-in-law had eight children, my father-in-law built this house with eight rooms, now all are locked. One of my sisters-in-law lives in a neighbouring village. She is also alone in her house. Her four sons are living in different towns. "Do you want Prakash to come to India"? "No, why should I want? Will he come, whoever went out of this village didn't come back. They didn't come even at festivals and ceremonies. His father used to say, he will not leave this village. I am the sole person left alone here. Let me show the lamp to every room as darkness has spread".

I followed her, she went ahead with a lamp in her hand and stopped at every door. After coming out, she told me this wooden bed belonged to the grandfather and the next one to his father. This verrandah was for men. She bowed before the two beds and asked me to do the same. I bowed before the two beds and restrained my laughter then she said, "Now let us go I will cook for you". "No I am not hungry, have just taken sweet porridge". "Was that enough?" she said, "Prakash would have taken twice, he likes milk products. His grandfather had four cows and the when two used to go dry, the other two used to give milk. Prakash's maternal grandmother sent one cow for him, our present cow is the granddaughter of that cow. She also is now old. "What will you eat, I will cook for you" I know how to cook rice, pulse and potato chips. She laughed, my son is strange and he has told you everything about my likes. I use to cook same things for Prakash as he liked.

Inspite of my objection she herself cooked food. She fed me and on my insistence, she took some food.

Next morning, I saw a stone antique in the yard, "what's this?" I asked, she said, it is a grinder, we use to get flour out of it. But now I also get from the machine, "Oh oh, this is an antique. I had organised two exhibitions of Indian antiques". "May be in America and Delhi you may have this name, but here we call it Janta, grinder". After some time, my hand was on the handle of this grinder, she put her hand above my hand and she also started moving it. She brought some wheat; she lifted the upper part of the machine and cleaned it. She put a fistful of wheat in it and started singing a song. Tears tickle down her cheeks, I could not understand the meaning of her song, I said, I will have the bread of this flour. She got up quickly and she prepared bread and vegetables for me. She taught me, the process of preparing vegetables and said, "Prakash likes these vegetables very much, you must learn to prepare it".

Next day, she was preparing halwa on putting ghee, she laughed, "Prakash used to call me miserly old woman. I put enough ghee in it", she wiped her tears and said, "I am remembering Prakash. He did not allow me to prepare halwa because you put small quantity of Ghee. "I will myself prepare it". He used to eat himself and feed me also. I was interested in her and thought she would be right person for my antique exhibitions in America, as she is a living and moving antique. At appropriate time I asked, if Prakash marries the girl of his choice, what you will do? "Nothing, he is nature from childhood, He will do everything after due consideration". I was surprised at her answer as Prakash used to say, "My mother will not agree. I can't marry the girl of my choice as my mom is very rigid".

Prakash was wrong, he could not realise the changes brought in last ten years. He considers himself modern, not a village man but there was no rigidness in his mother's mind, she said, "I am hardly a literate. I can read letter, my parents taught me that much". I can read letter from Prakash. I did not go even to Patna. How should I know about the world? When Prakash was going to America, the villagers told me, "He will marry there and not return. I did not believe this, but now I am forced to accept this. When he was studying in Delhi, his father settled his marriage, as a mother, I was happy as I had purchased few items for marriage ceremony. One even sicohora (wooden vermillion pot) and a Banarasi sari but he refused to marry. I still keep them with care". She showed me a rusted box and opened the lock of a rusted box. She started singing a village song regarding the marriage. Sometime she wept and laughed, she used to tell me about the household things as if she was my mother. She used to tell me the story of the couples of Sita Ram, Savirti Satyawan and examples of her own village. The whole day, village crowd was there. My interest in her went on increasing and by now I had a good knowledge of Indian village life. Ten days, I forgot the purpose of my coming, the innocence of the villagers made me a prisoner. I started thinking about calling back all Indians from America for the service of the motherland. I gathered courage and said, "Now I will go, you also have to go with me to America. Prakash has called you, "No, I won't go anywhere, I am alone in this house of eight rooms. If I go who will clean and light the house". She started to sing village folk. I understood the meaning of the folk song, she sang loudly, tears came to my eyes. The old mother laughed loudly and then she became calm and numb. I thought, I would make Prakash come back to India as India needs such brains, not America. The mother said, "Ask Prakash to come here once and you also keep coming, you will leave as my daughter. I have no daughter; with you I feel I am also mother of a daughter". After sometime she spoke again, "one thing worries me, how will Prakash come after my death. Village people may not be able to inform him".

She took me to a corner of the room and said, look here is a tin full of oil, when I die, I will tell the villagers to keep my body in this. As long as my son does not return they should not burn my body. She started weeping loudly, I also companied her as if both of us were mourning the death of Prakash's mother. You think, I am mad but I am not, and she kept silence. Time for my departure came, she offered me some gifts, she did not sleep the previous night. She kept a lamp burning and opening and closing some boxes. When I woke I found her writing a letter. At the time of departure she handed over a packet and red cloth for me. Again she began weeping and singing a folk song. At the time of departure, I was emotional and parrot was chanting, Prakash-Shivani-Prakash. When I reached Delhi, my mother said, how could you spend so many days in a village and you didn't bring Prakash mother. No she will not go, she is a unique character. Most state of the art antique. Prakash should come back to India. It took hours to describe Prakash's mother. I entered the bathroom and my mother opened the pack given to me. She kept the items on the center table. Coming out of the bathroom I said, "oh how beautiful is this banarasi sari, it's an antique sari". I was happy and I started examining the red sichora. His mother was saying that, son's mother keeps vermillion in this for daughter-in-law. My mother was reading the letter. I said what you have done, this letter is meant for Prakash, let me see it. I started reading the letter, "my son be blessed, you are still naughty and did not come to me and you have sent her, I liked your choice. May God bless you both? Once you must come to show me your face. The daughter-in-law will offer vermillion to village goddess. I have to feed sweet porridges to the villagers. Everybody in this village offers sweet porridges and I even received it. I am indebted to them, Shivani is a good girl. I have taught her many things; she can cook food of your choice. I spoke too much with her. Sometimes I realised that she would call me a chatter. She has known you by now but not more than me because I am a mother. Sometimes I feel that I don't know you, I have not told the villagers that Shivani would be you wife. She did not tell me, she lived with me as daughter. With blessings from your mother". What's this, Mummy did you read the letter? I was astonished. My mother said calmly, yes I have read. You will have to fulfil the wishes of the poor woman. You have also liked her very much, He will have to accept the choice of her mother. He will have to accept the choice of his mother as he is a devotee of his mother. I will talk to Prakash, "I think you will make a good couple, I was between the wheels of two mothers as my mother has no wishes. She talked to Prakash on telephone, he accepted without any conditions. I was tossing in the bed for whole night and I have condition for marriage as Prakash will have to come back to India to light the deserted eight room house in the village; to bring her son Prakash, to his mother's apron. Prakash is needed in India not in America.

□

## 5

# On the Marriage of a Child

Three decades have passed after the marriage of Shaeda, her two daughters have been married. She had grand children, now she is preparing for marriage of her third daughter. Her third daughter, Shakina looks after the household works. There are seven members in the family and the income is hardly two thousand rupees per month. So she had to cook twice, there is a tinned roof on the MLA flat. And sides are covered with old clothes instead of bricks. The members of the family bear the brunt of winter, summer and rain in the small place. They washed the clothes of clients and iron them. After a month, Shakina will marry and go to husband's house. I asked, "Now you have to cook the food?" "What can I do?" "But you are not yet old; women of your age in town are unmarried". I asked, "Will Shakina's husband take her to Calcutta". "No, he may take her to Calcutta sometimes. She will remain in the village and wash the clothes of the villagers. Village is big, people are affluent, and there is only one washer man family in the village. She will have to wash lot of clothes. The daughter of a washer man has no leisure either in fathers' house or at in laws place". "But you didn't live in the village; your husband brought you to town". There was appreciation of her husband in my words, Shaeda covered her face with her apron and said, "That is why my-mother-in law was angry with her son. She used to say "had she been beautiful, he would always take her to places, shameless, he takes her to cinema. I asked, "Why you are not good looking", she said, "I am jet-black, as black as the back of a earthen pot which is put on oven again and again, that is the reason my mother-in-law said so". Shaeda had milky white teeth, she had no grudge against her black skin, she was proud of her self. I asked, "Why did he marry a black woman"? She said, "My aunt initiated the discussion with him, she used to live in the same village. He asked his aunt, show me the girl, She was going to collect grass for animals. She said, "She is the girl, she is washing clothes on the bank of the river". Go and see her, He came to me and he said, "would you wash my pant", I was alone. My mother had cautioned me many times, while washing clothes don't speak to unknown person. And if there is man don't look at him. I kept looking down and told him, there are many washing logs. "Why have you come to me? I won't wash your clothes. Go away". "I have to get it washed soon", he said. "I won't wash your cloth in any way, don't waste my time. My mother may be coming, if she finds unwashed clothes, she will be angry at me. On the other hand, if she finds me talking to you, she will beat me". He went away. He didn't go to any other washer man's place. I kept looking at him; He also turned at looked at me many times". I thought he was a notorious, later on I came to know and told his mother, he wanted to marry me. His mother said, you shameless fellow, get out from the house, I had told you just to see her. After sometime, she said, "Ok tell me, you liked the girl". "She is good but bit rigid", Mother asked, "Is she as black as me"? "She is bit slim and homely girl, she will cook and wash clothes and help you in washing and ironing". He liked me and the marriage was performed. There was sign of victory on her face, "How old you were then", I asked, "Don't know, my breast had not come up yet". Removing her apron from her breast she said, "Even now, my breast is not visible, even after six children have sucked it to the last drop". She closed her breast with the apron. On the day of marriage, I got new clothes and some ornaments and good food to eat. This was enough for my happiness. He was quite adult at the time of marriage. He came to his village with enough money and told his mother, He would go to see his wife. His mother said, "You shameless, how you would go to see her without *gaona*, what will people of the village say". He was adamant and didn't take food for two days. His mother relented and said, "You rascal go but don't go straight to her house, first visit your aunt's place and send message from there, if your mother-in-law send message for you then go there. You are going crazy for marriage". He took sweets in earthen pot and sent the message through the son of my aunt. My mother and I were going to wash clothes and that time he came with the message. My mother became angry and said, "My son-in-law is so ignorant. He doesn't know that he can't see his wife before gaona, why so hurry? And how is her mother, he sent her son". "All newly married boys are like these and the duty of the mother is to restrain them. She has made us a laughing stock". After a pause, my mother said, go and tell my son in law, he should come for gaona and take her home. My aunt son returned bare handed, I asked, "You might have felt bad, your husband was turned away and not allowed to meet". Shaeda replied, "What husband, what wife, why should I feel bad? When my mother was expressing her anger, I had tasted four rasgollas, she turned to me and served some slaps on my cheeks and having gulped two rasgolla in my mouth, I ran to river side".

I had washed some clothes, suddenly a man came before me and said, "Please wash my shirt, I remember the incident happened a year back. I replied "No", He said, "You have to wash now, as you are my wife". I wanted to run away from there, I glimpsed and saw no body was there. I was afraid, I tried to run away. But he caught hold of my wrist, and hold it strongly. I told him, "Leave me, my mother may be coming. She will beat both of us". He reluctantly released me and gave a ten rupee note to me. I liked meeting him. I reached home, wanted to have some rasgollas but I found earthen pot broken outside my house. I was angry as I could not get rasgollas any more. I don't know why, earthen pot and the rasgolla in it and the sender of pot all seemed close to me. That ten rupee note had drawn closer to me. "What happened next", what was to happen, I wanted to see him. In six months ten rupees were spent, I remember the taste of the rasgollas, I waited for him to tell would you wash my pant. After a year, gaona was performed, I went to my mother-n-laws house. My mother-in-law was strict. She used to comment, "Your mother sent back my son, and she didn't allow him to see his wife. Perhaps you were very beautiful as white as milk, like English lady". As if my son touched you, the colour of the skin might have changed, you scoundrel". "Why did you tolerate torture of your mother-in-law"? She replied, "My husband used to tell me, don't reply to the words of my mother. Let her call you jet black, for me you are a beautiful lady. I will take you to Patna, keep your eyes and ears shut for some time". And you believed in him, "Yes, he used to speak from his heart, he brought me to Patna and he put me into servant's quarter of a minister. He used to wash the clothes and take it to the Minister's house. In the evening he used to bring jalabei or snacks. He loved me so much that I forgot my mother's house. He used to take me to village and bring back at intervals. "When a lady is loved by her husband, who can dare to scold her". But when you gave birth to four daughters, he might have been angry with you, "No-no, my husband is made of another metal. He is not like others. At the birth of my fourth daughter, he said, she is gift of God, don't dishonour her. Pandit ji of a Shiv Mandir said, "Daughters are Goddess of wealth". All though four Goddesses of wealth were born in my house, there was no wealth in my house. Ultimately Allah gave me two sons, my husband said, "Under go operation, don't trouble your body now". I was afraid of operation, but he got it done. It means you are loved by your husband, she was serious, "yes" she said, "That is so, he never wants to see my sad face. It because of him, I used to get early in the morning". How is that? There is always great pain in my waist. One day, we were coming back from cinema house and fell from the rickshaw, we survived but I hurt my back. Every morning, he massages my waist, only than I can leave the bed. "Bravo, you are very fortunate", "You are right". He tells, if Shakina goes, he can cook the food. Don't worry, children come to parent like flood water and go away. Family starts with husband and wife, don't weep. Not even at the departure of Shakina. But I can't accept this, after all I am a mother. I have given birth to this child. I may weep, but can't show my sad face to my husband. He says, keep smiling always. I have no money but I try to keep you happy. This is correct, money alone can't give happiness.

For me he is God, my mother-in-law didn't like my black colour so she wanted her son to marry again but he didn't agree. After the birth of my third daughters, my mother-in-law selected a girl for his remarriage. He didn't agree, he said, "Man or woman should marry only once". My mother-in-law made the selected girl, third wife of his brother. He left going to his aunt's house. How can I shed tears before such a man? But I can't hold tears for my daughter Shakina. She tried to hide her tears, she said, "My husband is a servant of God, a good man". Tears came to my eyes, she asked, why are weeping, "are you weeping for Shakina", "No not for Shakina, her marriage and congeal life is still to flourish. May God give him the good husband as yours, these tears are of happiness. I hope Sheeda should be as fortunate as you, everybody should get husband like yours. You are very fortunate. May you have ever lasting married life". She said, "Mami ji, I also practice Teej for my husband. It is a ritual for conjugal life. This ritual is for same husband for seven lives. You put on vermillion also. There is no practice of vermillion in your community, married women don't use vermillion, they put on burqa. You do not put on even that". Mami ji time has changed, Hindu and Muslim live together. They learn from one another, "Will the groom put on vermillion on the head of Shakina? "No after Nikha, some married woman will put vermillion on her head. It is decoration of the head", she said. Now she was alert, "Now I must go. Shakina father is calling, I have to iron clothes. I folded the clothes and pass on to him. The truth is that he always wants to see me before him". In a low voice she said, "Fact is that man is weaker than woman. He can't live without woman, we can live alone. He is always calls "Shakina's mom, Shakina's mom." I asked him – "Are you afraid to be comely?" You think! She gave many points to think and left me. Her wisdom and courage made me bow to her. The story ends but my work begins. The work is to tell the story of Sheeda to every house. To spread the story of her happy conjugal life. Every couple remember their marriage at the time of their children's marriage. Couple like Sheeda rain blessings on others. "May your conjugal life be good as mine."

□

# 6

# Not Disposable

That year also the flood was on high side. Everybody was heard saying, "have never seen such a flood". Supporting Ram Lalla, Jagdeo Singh also expressed surprise, Nanku was also not behind. Government may have many criteria for deciding the scale of flood but Ramsakhi had the steps of her house to predict the heights of flood. The year in which the house was built, all the seven steps of the house were under water. After the flood, the yard was raised by filling soil, now six steps were left. Every year the space was filled with soil and the flood would wash it away.

When Gouri came to this house, she was very eager to see the flood. "I never saw flood in my village and when I came here there was no flood for two years. I like to see the flood very much and enjoy boating". Gouri had heard from her father the description of the flood. When she was married in a village, prone to floods, she was very anxious. Before the marriage she heard, how water came to inner courtyard of the houses. It remained there for days snakes and different species of insects used to creep in the houses. She was afraid hearing that report. People used to spend time on the roof of the house and sometime food was dropped by helicopter. People used to ease themselves from the boats but she was very much interested to hear women riding boats and singing songs.

Even after two years of marriage she didn't see anything like that. Floods came but it remained limited to Bhartua Chour and then returned. After the third year of her marriage, flood started to wash the steps of her house. Every year one more step was covered by flood. That year the flood destroyed the paddy field and came up to the fourth stairs of the house. The people were in trouble, the big house of Jagdeo Singh turned into a relief camp. All the houses in the neighbourhood were under water. Her kitchen was always active. Gouri was happy, she said, "How lively is our house". Her mother in law was surprised at her simplicity and remarked, "Their houses have been flooded, and crop has been washed away. The food stored in the houses has been destroyed. They are in trouble. May god prevent such situation in future." Gouri's brother was employed in Delhi. He invited Gouri to Delhi on the occasion of Holi festival. Before accepting the invitation, she got it assured from her brother that she would be back before floods. This year flood was severe. Her four rooms were filled with water. The water entered her house in the darkness of midnight. She could not carry her necessary things to the roof of the house. They had to spend a week on the roof. Now flood was not a romance for her.

Ultimately the flood was over, but everything in house was soaked in water. Grains in mud (kothi) were soaked in water. So was the case with fire woods. It took many days to get the situation normalise. In course of arranging things, they found large number of unnecessary utensils. She asked her mother-in-law, "The old mud store with rejected goods has fallen down and goods are scattered. I will put them out and will call the vendor to sell them". His mother in law replied, "You do whatever you like, don't ask me". She didn't like to discuss, she was busy with taking out grains to dry them. She was helped by Paltu and her father-in-law. One day father in law was angry with his wife, "Have you gone senseless, has the flood come for the first time, it comes every year and has done its work. Get up and help your daughter-in-law". Next morning Gouri called Paltu, "Go and bring basket from the verrandah". She had a big basket of bamboo twigs, in which old utensils were stored. She wanted Paltu to carry on his head but he could not do it, he took two or three things at a time and kept them outside. Gradually he carried most of the things in instalment. Many things were dropped on the way, for instance a mat which she got from her father's house, this happened with her quilt too. The small and big utensils had lost their colours. Aluminium, bronze, brass lost their identity. Kohl pot and broken utensils were all collected together, Gouri asked Paltu and put them outside the gate. Let it be in sun for some time. Just clean them and call Mahesh, the vendor to sell them.

Paltu could not understand the meaning of selling the wastage. He put them into sun, it was the month of Bhado, and the sun was very hot. But the stain did not go. Gouri didn't put them back into the house. She had seen her sister-in-law in Delhi selling waste every month. If the newspaper were not kept properly, the buyer would not accept it or they pay very low price for it.

Her sister in law's sister-in-law had come from America. She told them what they did with waste material in USA. They put shoes, sandals, utensils, furniture and electronic goods outside their houses, whoever would need pick them up. She told them their many items in their household were picked from such waste.

Early morning Gouri told her mother in law, "I have kept all the waste, old broken things outside the house, have a look at them. I will call the vendor and sell them", Gauri expected her mother in law to say, "Do whatever you like", but it didn't happen so. Ramsakhi got up and went to the door, Gouri was busy in household work. After a long time she came to see her mother-in-law. Ramsakhi was sitting near the pile of waste material and staring at one of them. Gouri went to her and asked, "What happened, whatever you have to pick up, kindly do it, vendor is coming". Ramsakhi took a broken kohl pot and asked "Do you know when it came to our house and who brought it"? No I don't know, I am seeing it for the first time, "This kohl pot was brought by aunt(phua) of your father-in-law on his birthday. She applied kohl to the child, my father-in-law was very liberal. He registered 10 kathas of land to her sister for this kohl ceremony. He used to cultivate the land every year and send the price of the grains to his sister. After his death also the practice continued for two years. After listening to her family history, Gouri was lost in the Kohl pot, when the vendor came, he also was listening he story of land plot and he forgot the purpose of his coming there. After the Kohl pot touched another utensil, Ramsakshi got lost in the past and said, "Gouri, this unfortunate utensil is cause of the death of my son. It was the day of Holi. "I was preparing sweets (pua). My eight year old son came silently and took up a pua from the mud pot and ran away. He again came and tried to run away with one more pua, I didn't know his hand was in the pot and the hot instrument fell on his hand. He cried a loud, with a same hot instrument I bet twice-thrice on his back. His hand and back both were burnt because of this wound, he died after two months. Ramsakhi started to weep for the son who died four decades ago. The vendor saw this scene and he said "I will come tomorrow, now it's too late". Gouri requested the vendor to come next day. The vendor assured her and he collected his weighting machine, weight measurement and went away. Gouri asked her mother in law to get up wash her face.

Ramsakhi said, "Sit for some time." She had a bronze water pot in her hand. She was telling the story of bronze water pot. In the meantime Gouri's son came from the school with bag on his back. She asked, "Did you run away from the school early or did the teachers didn't come?" "The school was over at five, all the teachers had come." Gouri realised now that it was evening. She persuaded Ramsakhi to go inside the house, she was consoled and fed. After sometime Ramsakhi again went to the heap of waste material and picked up an item. It was evening, she had picked up a roti maker. This instrument was purchased by her grandmother in Laschigunpur mela. After two years of her marriage, it came to her. That village was rich, in rice so this roti maker was seldom used. Once in the month of June, there was fire in the village, her house was also burnt and this roti maker was half burnt. For several days vendor used to come to the house and listen to the stories of items. The flood had given a rise to the business of the vendor and had no time to listen to the story of Ramsakhi. In course of telling the story of utensils, Ramsakhi became healthier. The story of her childhood and youth revived her and there was no scope for getting her worry and sad. Ramsakhi was normal and Jagdeo Singh was very happy. A vendor came with his balance and sack together to purchase waste material. Gouri with the help of Paltu was using lemon juice for cleaning the utensils. The vendor said, "It's not necessary, no need to clean it. It will be melted and new utensils will be cast." Gouri said firmly, "No this will not be sold now. My mother in law is living because of them. The story of the family is related to these utensils. They are not waste material as they are priceless, you can't pay the price". Gouri was lost in them. After fourteen years, she was engrossed in the family history and she was happy. The vendor put his empty sack on the cycle and he murmured, "Now the daughter-in-law has drowned in flood of memories never save this housewife. I must go to some other house. May there also I hear the dialogue of mother-in-law and daughter in law reading their family history.

# 7
# A Mother of Countless Children

It was the first day of Parvati in the maternity ward. During the course of her training, she used to tell her friends, "I will never opt for service in the maternity ward". Her friend Maria asked, "Why". "I am the first child of my parents, after me, six siblings were born. At the time of birth of my sister, I never left my mother. I used to cry with her without knowing the reasons. Then one brother was born, I was now a grown up. My grand ma didn't allow me to go to the delivery room, I used to listen to her cries from the door. That is the reason I don't want to work in maternity ward". Parvati had expressed her desire firmly.

Parvati did not know that destiny will take her to the place, where she didn't want to go. There was no question of her likes and dislikes. Her younger sister, while studying in high school had married a person of her choice. Next five siblings were dependent on her earnings. She had to look after their future. The first day in the hospital was not comfortable for her.

The doctor asked her name, the room was empty. At that moment, four persons entered the room with a woman in labour pain.

The lady doctor asked the person to go out of the room and made her lay on the bed but the woman resisted. Lady Doctor looked at Parvati. She made the woman lay on the bed. The last loud cry of the woman was unbearable for Parvati. She left the room but when she had the first cry of the child, she ran into the room. Doctor asked her, "Separate the umbilical cord and wash her, you won't learn if you run away". Parvati gradually learnt the art and science of delivery and maternity process.

She used to tell her first experience to the new nurses. How she learnt every process. The touch of soft body of a new born child, gave a new feeling. After washing, she would roll the child in new cloth and put in mother's lap. The smile on the face of the mother was awesome and she had no fears now. She didn't run away from the room at the time of delivery and she was first to look at the child coming from the mother's womb.

The number of delivery cases was increasing, so ward was spacious and more staff was employed. At times, four or five beds were needed for delivery. The nurses have to stand before the patients. But other nurses before putting the new baby in the lap of mother, first put in Parvati's lap. This continued for many years. On the same bed, in the same room, mother's from various caste and creed used to deliver the children. All children were equal for her. In her lap, all children were equal. They were neither Hindu non Muslim; nor Sikh nor Christain. They could assume denominations once the babies go back in their mother's laps. Parvati never kept the head count of the children put in her lap. As a mother never counts the number of breads at the time of cooking.

This was teaching of her grandmother but Parvati never forgot to tell the new mothers, "Two are enough, get your operation done. You don't need more children. Children make you realise supreme happiness. God transfers his duty to mothers. Two children are enough to make you God". Sometimes mother used to come with her children to Parvati, Parvati was happy to touch them. Many women followed her words and got themselves operated. She used to caution them to take care and get all the vaccinations done timely.

She insisted on her brother and sisters' educated and helped them to get employed and now they are all married. But she never thought about her future. After the death of her mother, she thought about herself. But now she was almost fifty years old. Sometimes baby born with her hands used to come with their wife or husband. She was very happy, she used to get lost in the past and forget her future.

In that ward, the custom of putting every child on her lap continued. She used to examine the child thoroughly. If there was any deficiency, she would quickly run to the doctor. Many mothers would come to her and tell, "Your timely care saved my child that is why he is healthy today".

The first child of her hand was Samir, Parvati herself had given this name to him. Samir was now 35 years old. She didn't have to calculate her age, now it was time for her to retire. Now this made her worry, "where will I go now, I will have to vacate my government quarter".

In 35 years of her service, she didn't see any other part of Delhi. Her world was limited from nursing ward to quarters. The administration decided to extend her service for five years and the quarter for residence. After five years also, she continued coming to the ward. Nobody prevented her, she stayed in the nursing ward but she didn't have any salary for this. Thus twenty years passed by, she was now tired. She could not hold the child in her weak hands so she decided to discontinue this work. But before that she heard the pain of woman in labour. She went to her and put her hand on her hand. She started examining the time of delivery, she found a big black pot on her thigh, "are you daughter of Nirmala and your father is a police inspector". "Yes, but how do you know this, she was surprised to hear the name of her late mother".

"You were born by my hand, the spot on your thigh, I could recognise you. Has your mother come"? "No, my mother is no more my parents died last year in an accident. A new wave of pain came to the expectant mother, she started crying. Parvati put her hand on her face. In the meantime, another woman entered the room and asked, "How long will it take?" The nurse standing beside her said, "Only she will tell you", and the women looked at Parvati. "O you still come here, you have wonderful courage". "I think you are Arti? who is she to you? She pointed towards the woman in pain. "She is my daughter in law. Fifty years ago, I was born at your hands. Twenty six year ago my son Anurag was born and now my granddaughter is coming. Arti was over whelmed to see Parvati, she reminded her, "My maternal grandmother used to say that I was a pre matured child and might have died at the time of my birth but you saved me. For twenty days, I was kept in the hospital here and then my maternal grandmother took me home. When I was grown up, she got me married and Samir was also born at your hands. I hope you remember this". She remembers everything; she said, "You are the second child born at my hand. Samir was the first. After two years Kamalkanth was born, father of your daughter in law. He was a police inspector; this child is also born at my hand, what a co-incident." Arti remembered the face of her maternal grandmother. It will take at least three to four hours in the delivery. She is a woman with great patience. In the next three hours, many incidents were discussed. In the meantime, the expectant mother had delivered a girl child, she was washed and put in her lap.

Now it is enough. I won't come from tomorrow. Arti came back to her house and told Anurag in detail about Parvati, "she had no house of her own, the hospital itself was her own. Now she is very old, I will take you to her tomorrow. She will be very happy to see you. Next morning, they reached the hospital. They had to bring the child and mother back. She asked the nurse sitting there, "Where is Parvati Ji? She is not visible, I don't see her".

"I am also surprised, she had come here till last evening". Arti asked another nurse. She gave her the address of her house, Anurag was very anxious to see her. Arti said, "Today we will take Nirja and child home, tomorrow we will come to see her. We have to invite her to our home once". "Yes", Anurag said. Nirja was also searching for Parvati, she told her mother, "I cannot forget her touch, and she put her hand on my hand and my pain was immediately gone". Next day, Nirja reminded Anurag, "At the time of returning from office, bring Parvati with you". By evening Anurag reached the house, he kept knocking at the door, there was no sound inside, no lock on the door, gradually people gathered there. The door was forcibly opened, we were stunned. The lifeless body was sitting in the chair. Someone informed the hospital and many nurses came quickly. One of the nurses said, we should inform her relatives. The other nurse said, "We don't know who are her loved ones. There are families of her brother and sister but we don't know her address". The third nurse said, "What's the necessity for searching anyone". Anurag undertook the situation, he said, "let her be here, I will search for her close ones". They agreed to his proposal. Her body was laid on ice. In the age of information revolution, wonders happen. Anurag mind was quick. He devised a strange advertisement. "All those were born in the AIIMS hospital between 1955 to 2005 may kindly gather in 22 Sarojini Nagar. Your mother Parvati, the nurse is no more, her death procession will take place on 2nd January from 22 Sarojini Road to Lodhi cremation centre." The notice by email, website and blog and poster reached large number of people. This was advertised in the newspaper also.

This unmarried women and had hundreds of children; it was a unique procession. Parvati herself was unique. The last rites were performed by Anurag and large crowd gathered to put wood on pyre. Parvati had inspired emotions in hundreds of people. She was mother of innumerable children. On the Ghat, Arti told her son, "You have done the right thing. I am your mother who gave birth to you but she gave you the first touch. I will remain mother of one son and one daughter; she was the mother of hundreds of children. Her status will remain superior to me. She will bless you and those who have come here.

□

# 8
# Kaki's Pilgrimage

That was not the first pilgrimage of kaki. She was a regular visitor to holy places. She had visited Ayodha, Mathura, Kasi, Jankapur and Ganga Sagar. Pilgrimages to these places made her leader amongst women going to pilgrimages. She would take group of village women without any help from any man. Sometimes she would go alone, even young women were permitted to go on pilgrimage with her.

Kaki was very popular in the village. Out of 365 days, she used to spend almost 100 days out of the village. She would return from one pilgrimage and very soon preparations for another would begin. Every journey had some new good or bad experiences; she would learn from experiences. Once a pick pocket took away her money; she changed the design of her blouse. While alighting from her train, her long hair were entangling in the gate. In next journey, she shaved her hair. In another journey the mouth of the bag was opened and hence something fell down, she started tying a knot on the bag. Her co-travellers used to follow her orders strictly also they would be dropped next time. If a woman had not been permitted to go to her father's house for a long time, she would say, "She is prisoner for four years, this time I will take her for a dip to the Ganges". If some women used to vex her mother in law she would say, "I will take you to Ganga Sagar this time and your daughter-in-law will learn a lesson as how to run household without you". Whenever she used to return from pilgrimage she would bring bags full of gifts for members of the family. Mother would bring warm water for her, my aunt would wash her and help her in bath and feed her. Women of the whole village would surround her cot, one by one some would massage her body. She would bless them, she would give sweet balls to married women. She would bring tulsi garland for widows and small statute of Gods. Women were interested more in her stories of pilgrimage than in gifts.

Once she was going to Tirupati. On the way, she met many pilgrims. She didn't understand their languages. Two young men came and occupied the seat. She was sitting on the floor. She abused the boys in her language. They kept laughing at her. She thought now she should talk to them softly, she said, "I am your Aaji", the boys left the seat quickly and asked her to sit and they served him throughout the journey. According to her, boys belonged to "Andhara Pradesh" (Andhra Pradesh). Her talk made everybody laugh. She said, "What can I do, sometimes I meet people from Karkat (Karnataka), sometime from Madarass (Madras).

For her there was no difference between her village and other places. For her Kanpur, Nagpur, Jalandhar, Jaipur were all pardes. But people are same everywhere. She used to say, "Although languages are different, they understand me." Kaki had become a social worker, she used to fix marriages of many girls at the holy places and she would inform the guardians of the girls after coming home. Nobody had the courage to reject her proposal. Having heard sermons of saints and mahatmas, she had become a religious teacher. She would tell the story of Ramayan, Bhagwad Gita, Sukhsagar to everybody. If she met some good sadhus at a holy place, she used to invite them to her village, "come to my village, your sermon will be useful to villagers, and they will stop fighting. Village will turn into a heaven".

With the help of villagers, sermons of sadhus were organised. This made her very happy, "my village has become Ayodha, Mathura, Kasi". She used to follow the teachings of Mahatmas. There was no untoucability in the village. No mother-in-law would torcher her daughter-in-law. No man had the courage to beat his wife, she had a good knowledge of good and bad of sadhus. If she found some sadhu fake, she would disrobe his saffron cloth and make him wear ordinary clothes. "Shameless man, afraid of work, lives on alms, take this spade, dig my field and I will feed you". For days she used to force to dig his field and fed him. People of the village used to help her on such occasions. She used to say, you call me *'Musafir Kaki'*. Everybody is a traveller, when time for death comes, travelling ends. That is why, I say; follow good path. You have to go from where you have come. Everybody would listen to her attentively. They would say, "She speaks like Mahatma, others would say that, she was not less than a Mahatma. By frequent pilgrimages, she had become a Mahatma. After every pilgrimage, she would bring some new message to the village. After tasting idli, she would share her flat rice and homemade pooris with others. Sometimes she would talk of *Sarso ka Sag and Makka ki Roti* and sometime she would *dal bati choorma with litti. Idli and dosa* were new to her, they were just *bagaya and chawl ki* roti.

Kaki had been to Ganga sagar. On return, she was informed that her parrot had died. People thought that she would cry for her beloved parrot. Kaki said, "The time for leaving with me was over. I met a sadhu in Ganga Sagar. He used to say all relations in this world is like floating logs of wood in the river. By chance, they come together and separate". Kaki was illiterate but she collected all the leaflets from holy places. She would ask village youth to read them.

Maha Kumbh was organized in Haridwar, Kaki started preparing for journey. I also decided to go with her, she said "no I won't take you with me". "Why?", "You are quiet young, time is bad, now I am old I can't look after you. I don't know when my life journey will end". She had to bow to my wishes, before going to Haridwar; she visited every house in the village. All villagers came to bid farewell to her. There was big gathering of people with her. I was the youngest of them all. While seating in the train, she tied one end of her sari at her waist and the other end, she tied to my waist. On my objection she said, "Be silent and follow my orders". When we reached Haridwar, it was full of tents. There was no place for our stay. Kaki arranged things quickly, Sadhu of Srignaeri Mutt had occupied a big plot. One of them recognized Kaki and said, "Come and stay with us", "we are not alone", "no matter come all of you". We all settled there. Early morning, we used to go for bathing in Ganga. She never forgot to tie her waist with mine. She used to sing prayers in loud voice and we used to follow her. Either people from Andhra or Karnataka, all understood song from Kaki, everyday sermons were delivered by Shankracharyas. At night, sometimes kaki used to sing her prayers. People would put mike before her. A large crowd used to gather, listening to her songs. One day, Shankracharya ji was overwhelmed. Kaki was singing, Sita's character. She would compose some poems in Maithili on the spot. She would move every heart by singing Samadavan.

"Song sung at the time of departure of a daughter, kaki would move with her group in the mela. She used to listen to the sermons of sadhus and saints. One day, she found an old woman, separated from her group and next day she found a child away from his group. She would search for their group and send them back.

On Next day, main bath was to be held. Nagas and Shankarcharyas were first to take their groups for bath. Kaki didn't sleep for whole night, early morning she left for bath, singing songs for Ganga maiya. The procession went on increasing; our group got stuck in the crowd. The crowd was motionless kaki started singing 'Ram Nam' loudly. She released the sari tied to my waist and forced me to climb the platform. "No, I will not leave you, she shouted "go up" and she also shouted at police man, "pull her up, she is my grand daughter. Take care of her, I will come and take her back." Police man pulled me up, a great crowd pushed from behind. Kaki was taken away and with her lot of other people, I shouted at the top of my voice "Kaki-kaki", but my voice didn't reach her. By the time I reached there, her voice was lost; I caught hold of her body and began crying. A sadhu came to me and said, get up now! Your kaki is no more. Now she won't listen to you any more, you have to perform her last rites. I could not understand anything, an old man from my village said, "How is it possible? She is a girl." The sadhu smiled, what's the difference between a girl and a boy. Your Musafir Kaki was a woman, she used to take care of all of you, is there any man equal to her in your village?" As if Kaki was guiding us, he is true saint accept what he says.

I performed last rites advised by the sadhu, people from Andhra, Karnataka and saint and sages from everywhere participated in her last journey. The journey of Musafir Kaki ended on the bank of ever flowing Ganges.

□

# 9

# Delaying Divorce

Harsh was surprised at the proposal of Vishaka, as usual she had expressed herself in loud and harsh word as if they were not words but bombs and it has busted. Harsh had not heard these words. He was afraid of meaning of the words. He had never spoken such words, his close friends Sikander has once pronounced the unfortunate word thrice and his relation with Salma ended. Harsh used to think that there are many words which are used as abusive and people speaking them are considered uncivilized but they don't harm anybody. May be for sometime the word makes the speaker tongue foul and hurt the listener. But there is no change in their relations. The word spoken without intention changes the relationship of the individuals. The relation was disrupted; Salma started striking her head against the wall. The word spoken thrice changes the status of a woman. The most devoted Salma turned into nothingness so he was afraid of this word, whose result was fearful. Harsh and Sikander were close friends from childhood. They never felt the feelings of being different community but that day, Harsh was greatly relieved to realize himself of a different community. In his society, the word spoken thrice doesn't destroy the relation, he returned home but his mind was still at Sikander's house. He saw Salma in desperate condition. Vishaka wanted to know what had happened.

He was out of trance; he looked at his newly married wife Vishaka and he gave a big hug to her. This untimely behaviour surprised her, for the whole night Harsh was doing something new with her. He kept her close to his chest for the whole night. He would keep her face in his hands and stare at her. This unexpected behaviour made Vishaka restless. In the morning, when Vishaka left her bed, he caught hold of her arms she said, "What are you doing, what has happened to you?" Harsh was not ready to confess the fact which made him behave like that but Vishaka ultimately forced him to tell the truth. She knew that Sikander has broken the relation with his wife by saying the word 'Divorce' thrice. Vishaka's kind-hearted husband could not tolerate the sight and she tried to console and mentally support her husband.

Almost two years, and their passionate emotions subsided. The reality of conjugal life appeared before them. Vishaka was very angry, everyday a new complaint arose in her mind and a big list was prepared. Some complaint appeared in Harsh's mind also. He told his problems before his friend, they said its usual.

Harsh had seen his parents fighting and whole house used turning into battle ground but next morning treaty of peace would be signed. This situation has not come in the life of harsh. He tried to change himself, Vishakha also tried to fulfil the duty of conjugal rights. One day Vishakha was very angry and she expressed the words, "I want divorce from you, I can't live with you any more".

He could not sleep for the whole night. Next day Harsh couldn't work properly in the office. Very frequently he used to press the mobile number of Vishakha. He knew that Vishaka, would not come from office at 4 pm even then he came back home. Without Vishaka, house was a place of ghost for him. Vishaka in house would go on chattering. She would scold him, she would fight with him. Sometimes he would leave the house and go out.

That evening Harsh returned before time. The harsh sound of the call bell used to annoy him. One day Vishakha had asked him, "Why don't you purchase a call bell with a sweet sound? Suddenly the call bell rany, he opened the door but before him was the daughter of washerwoman with clothes. He placed the clothes and shut the door and prepared tea and again the bell rang. When he opened the door, a woman with plastic bag, full of vegetables was standing before him. The woman was surprised to see Harsh instead of his wife at that time.

This was the time of Vishaka to be in the house and she had fixed time with domestic helpers. Harsh got a wave shock "As was the time for the Vishaka to be in the house, why she was in the office? May be, she has gone to consult some lawyer about the divorce threat she has given. She can't take divorce and can't live without me. Although she was employed in a private company, her salary is not enough. Harsh got her admitted to MBA by correspondence and once she completes it, she could get a good job. He remembered Vishaka had the key to the flat. Why should she press the call bell? At that very time the door opened and Harsh hid himself in a corner. Having entered, she saw the clothes and bag with vegetables placed on center table. She guessed Harsh might have come home, she read her watch. She was late in coming and did not try to search for Harsh and in a flux he appeared before her. He said, "You are late in coming today", "yes, the boss gave me some extra work, so had to finish it before coming home".

Harsh believed that Vishaka had forgotten her proposal for divorce. He was apprehensive that she would repeat the proposal. Next week when she repeated her proposal for divorce, Harsh said, "You are not in position to take divorce, you have to stand on your own, must have a house of your own". One day he said, if you have decided to live separately, you have to be prepared for it. Vishaka kept calm, she kept hearing him. He had a scheme to set her on her own legs as a father thinks about his children. Vishakha passed MBA and with his initiatives, she got a job in new company with higher salary. Fact was that Vishaka was annoyed with official work of Harsh. He would go to the office at 9 am and come by 5 pm. Harsh used to spend lot of time in the office, this made her loneliness unbearable. She decided to remain separately. At least she will not have to wait for him in the other house. I want divorce as soon as possible. Harsh was examining the papers of flats, he had booked for Vishaka. So he did not give much importance to her word. Harsh was dreaming of a new flat, TV, microwave, dining table and a car for her. It was as if he was not divorcing with his wife but trying to settle a daughter. Harsh used to talk about his scheme for settling Vishaka to his friends and they used to laugh and make fun of him. He did not care for that. Vishaka also did not care; his liberality was like a burden to her. That evening Harsh had brought many kitchen gadgets. Vishaka was very angry. She did not like his sympathy, out of anger she said, "What is the necessity of purchasing these things?" Did you purchase utensils for this house; you did not help me in settling this house, why did you extend help in breaking the house. If you have brought everything, why did not you bring a cradle, I will now need that. Harsh was full of life, the words from Vishaka filled his heart with happiness. She informed him, he was happy. He had wished Vishaka to have a child before separation. He never forced himself on her but it was God's mercy in the expectation of child coming, they would live for nine months together. The new situation of coming of the child made flat lively, friends used to come frequently. Harsh used to return home early and play with Shivam. This made Vishaka glad. He thought Vishaka had forgotten the idea of divorce. One evening she said, "I haven't forgotten of divorce from you, I want divorce from you. At that time Shivam was in the lap of Harsh, Shivam started crying. It was beyond his power to keep the child quiet. He gave Shivam to Vishka. He stopped crying, Harsh wanted to play with him again but Vishaka didn't gove Shivam back to him. For the whole night, Harsh kept analysing the cry of the child. Why did he cry when Vishakha talked of divorce from husband? May be the child didn't like the parents to be separated. Harsh had heard that children are incarnation of God, perhaps God don't like separation of parents but there was no looking behind. Vishaka had decided to live separately and both had no time to talk to each other it was because of their his time. Now Harsh had also decided, there is no purpose of living together. He has seen in his house, his grandmother and aunts. Their main purpose in life was to keep their husband happy. In last few decades situation had changed, women have taken to jobs in office. They don't have time to care for her husband and children. Harsh understood this, that if two people can't live happily under one roof, they should live separately. He wanted Vishaka to go to her flat as soon as possible. But Harsh was getting attached to Shivam, he had learnt calling papa.

It was month of March; Harsh would come home by midnight, a few nights, he did not come home. The behaviour of Vishakha made him think that she would again repeat her proposal. He told his wife, "I have lot of work in office, next week I will take leave from office and arrange your new flat".

Vishaka did not reply. She took Shivam and went to her office. He was now used to be kept in the crèche. From next day, Harsh went on leave for a week. That morning Vishaka did not prepare for crèche and left him playing with Harsh. At the time of her leaving for office, Harsh asked, will Shivam not go to crèche today? No the crèche is closed today and you are not been on leave otherwise, I would have taken him. Harsh was very happy, he kept playing with his son. For a few days the crèche was closed and so he kept playing with Shivam. Harsh used to look after his son Shivam and in between find time for packing for the new flat.

Next day his leave was to be over, Harsh asked her, "Give me the key to that flat, I will set all the things there". At the time of Vishaka going to office he said, "A paper of divorce has been prepared by lawyer. If you return early we will go together", she didn't utter a word. She went to her office, Harsh was anxious as he had to go office early morning. He had looked after Shivam for a week. Vishaka came back from office early in the evening and had two packets with her. Harsh said, "You change the dapper of Shivam, I will prepare tea. And you have to go to the pleader". "Why don't you take tea, you should not delay". This made him happy that his wife cares for him. Both were taking tea in the balcony silently Vishaka broke the silence. There was farewell organised for me in the office. They have given me some presents would you see them? "What farewell, Harsh was surprised how will she leave alone without job. Vishaka opened her small packet, how beautiful are these tea mugs so that two persons sitting together may sip tea for long time. Harsh did not show any interest in the mug. Vishaka took out a paper and offered it to Harsh, she had sold the flat to some of her friends. Harsh shouted, "What have you done, will you live on the roads". Vishakha replied calmly, "I will live in this flat, will live like wife and husband. You will earn and I will enjoy. The expense on crèche and nanny will be saved. Harsh was numb. He thanked God and he took up Shivam and pressed him against his chest. He was a father now, formerly a babysitter. It took time for him to realise the delay of divorce.

□

# 10

# Adopted Father

A month back, he had received a letter from an Old Age home, Haridwar. It informed him about his father Mahendar Singh's illness. He was upset at this information. His mother was no more; he could not see her at the time of her death. He remembered his childhood, a small courtyard and his mother sitting before oven and his three sisters sitting together. He would remember, his father's words, "How many times I told you not to jump on the cot. If it's broken you will have to sleep on the floor". His father was a teacher with a meagre income. He had purchased a cycle, all these memories were vivid to him. He had read in childhood, "the memory of bad days gives us happiness in good days and memory of good days hurts in bad days."

His 60th birthday was coming, he was not so much happy to visualize his future. He had achieved success one after another, in last 30 years. Away from his country and his people. He didn't find time to look back.

He was engaged in assessing the positive and negative sides of his life. He had amassed so much of wealth and property that generations could survive without doing anything, so local people were envious of him. He had built big bungalows for his children; everybody was busy in himself. Perhaps this is why he was thinking of his people and happy memories of the past.

He used to quarrel with his sisters Sunita, Shymala and Sujata. Under one quilt, the whole family would spend the night in cold days. Now grew his desire to know about his ancestors, who had shaped his mind and body; who where his father and great grandfather.

His grandfather was a great religious person of his area. In this country, nobody cares as to what his ancestors were, a dacoit or a smuggler. He was known here as S.N. Singh not Siddarth Singh. His identity was only Mr. Singh. In last 50 years he had worked like a donkey. Now he wanted to enjoy the family tradition. He was proud of his intellectual and achievements. Suddenly he decided to go to India, He didn't tell his wife Sarla, she was busy in her own world. That made him more lonely.

He decided to see his father. When he came to International airport at Delhi, no one was to receive him there. The moment he came out of the airport, he touched mother earth with his head. He had changed in last 50 years. He hired a Taxi and started towards Haridwar. He saw changes taken place in the countryside. When he reached the Ashram, he found a name plate hanging from the door. Shri Mahendra Singh, age 80, village Bilsalpur. Inside the room, a body on the cot was being examined by doctors and nurses. The doctor and others were surprised; they asked him to keep quiet. The patient on the cot had been silent for last two days. He had left taking food and water. They were trying to persuade him to take food. "I am Siddarth, your son, father I am Sidhu, have come from America". He shouted in his ears, as if a new life had come into the old body, he spoke, "where are you Sidhu; you have been late in coming. The old man lost his consciousness in his arms. This news quickly spread to the Ashram. The old inmates felt as if their own son had come. In the son's company the old man revived.

Five years ago, a letter had reached from Sujata to Siddarth, "Amma is no more, she aboded to heaven while taking your name. Now father is alone, all sisters requested him to come to their house. But he was not ready to leave in the house of his daughters. What can I do, please come at least once". But Siddarth could not come.

The old man used to talk about his children's childhood. He was surprised at the memory of his father, he was also a father, but he didn't remember in detail childhood of his children. He remembered once his father was sitting on Harki Pauri, and he was taking bath in the Ganges. For some time, he was under water. His father shouted, "Save – save my child". Many people jumped to search for the child, then he surfaced on the water. "O! I have got my son, many thanks to Almighty Ganges". All the people there had a big laugh; he scolded him, "Don't tease me". You remembered once you had a big abscess on your back. This made you cry a lot. For six months, we consulted doctors, it was not cured, ultimately your mother got you to Haridwar, and she took bath in Ganges and prayed for you. Within months your wound healed. I was afraid, whether your mother fulfilled her promise to Almighty Ganges or not. "But Ganges is also mother and she pardons mistakes". Your mother very much remembered you. She wanted to touch your body before her death. She was as pious and as religious as Ganges. He used to go to Ganges for bath every day, sometimes he used to take his father to river.

One day, large number of people at the courtyard at the temple considering it proper occassion, Siddarth said, "I will take my father with me". This made everybody silent; many people had gone back with their family members. He knew that, ashramites will not allow him to take the old man with him. What happened are you all right, Hari Kishore Singh said, I am not your father, Siddarth was stunned, what mistake did I make, I don't want to leave you alone. I have to return to America. Hari Kishore Singh was in a mess, he has spent his life as a free man. He had no attachment with his parents and sisters. So his father had decided to get him marry at the age of 16. On the day of marriage, he rode a horse but the horse instead of going to bride house went somewhere else and this changed his life forever. He was a freedom fighter and India gained independence. Now he was a member of a national organisation, he had no lust for family relations. He spent his youth and adulthood without any family, but childhood and old age need some help at both these stage of life. Now that he was ageing, he needed rest and a new culture had developed in the society, the culture of Old Age Homes. He was admitted in one of them; There his roommate was Mahendra Singh. He was attached to his son, day and night he would tell stories about his son, and ultimately Hari Kishore Singh also got attached to his son. The similarity in their shape and size made people call them twin brothers. May be like Hindi films they were separated in childhood and again met in old age. After death of Mahendar Singh, this realisation was more intensive. Both of them were like two bodies and one heart as in case of twins, if one was unwell other would follow. He also decided to follow death but arrival of Siddarth changed this misfortune, he was also enjoying intimacy of a son. He took out a diary from his bed and handed it over to Siddarth said, "This diary belongs to your father. You are on every page of his diary. This diary for me is like Gita and Ramayana. Your father became Krishna and Dushrath for me. Take this and read, your father in this diary and not in my face". As an obedient son, he started turning page of this diary. In course of helping the old buddy, it never came to his mind that he was not his real father. After reading the diary, he became more sure that man sitting before him was the character in the diary.

It is true that a child and an old man have common features. An old man is like a child. It is difficult to differentiate between two new born babies. Siddarth took the old man as his own father. Nobody in the Ashram made any grudge against him, after all an inmate of the ashram had survived without medicine. Ashramite knew that for last five years, Harikishore ji and Mahendar ji had become one, only fifteen days ago, Mahendar Singh took abode to heaven and Hari Kishore ji, decided for self death. He refused water and food, had Siddarth delayed his arrival, he wouldn't have seen, the prototype of his father; he would have returned barehanded. Hari Kishore ji affectionately said, "Siddarth you didn't remember your father, even at the birth of your son. Every young man when becomes father remembers his father. You father used to be very anxious at the time of your birth". Siddarth started weeping; he was himself a discarded father. It was long time that he had seen his father, last time he came to India at the time of his sister's marriage, Sujata. He had requested his parents to come to America with him, they could not give up their attachment to the small house and ancestor's place. Sometimes he used to receive letter from his father and sisters, perhaps the relatives were tired. Relations are kept alive by exchanging ideas and letters.

It was about a month that he was enjoying company of the old man that is why he has proposed to take him to America. His demand was so strong that nobody could refuse it. But the question was that he was not the blood relation of Siddarth. All the law books were consulted. This was a beginning of a new culture. He could adopt him as his father. At the time of departure everybody blessed him, all the old men there wished, somebody would also take them away from Ashram. A new era, began in the life of Hari Kihore ji, he got a new sky and Siddarth a new earth. He got a father of course a Adopted One.

□

# 11

# Warmth of Touch

It was not for the first time that Raj Kumari ji was in bed. Till 70, she has been helping and serving her own people and others. She has helped many individuals through her appointed doctors and nurses. She is neither a doctor nor a nurse, but in course of taking ill persons to doctors and the doctor's prescription to ill people, she had learnt many names of diseases. People from the village used to come to her and she would give a patient hearing to them. She would take her phone and call the doctor saying, "I am sending a patient, kindly examine him properly and consider him as a member of my family". It was not for the first time that she was telling this to the doctor, she has been taking hundreds of patients to the doctor's treatment and Raj Kumari Ji's kind words made soothing effect on the patient. The patient would thank her and bless her children and went home. She always talked to her friends about the patient's and the doctors who helped them fight their diseases. She herself suffered many small diseases and she recovered from them. But some diseases made permanent abode in her body. The present was something very serious. When I telephoned her, her voice was weak. I asked, "What happened?", "I am not well for last two months" "oh! I didn't know". I had telephoned her to help some patient from Bihar. He had requested me to telephone Raj Kumari Ji because she has helped his father when he was unwell. I told the patient, Raj Kumari Ji herself in bed, "I am going to see her. If I find her better, I will talk about you". The patient also started praying for her quick recovery, I reached Raj Kumari's house; her condition was bad. The doctor was examining her and some women relatives had surrounded her. I sat down in a corner. After the doctor left, she called me, "why you phoned me, is there any patient to be examined in the medical institute, what is he suffering from". "I told her, no there is no patient". She knew that I telephoned her not without purpose, I could not ask in detail about the disease. I asked, "where is Gonu?" "Today she has gone to school, and she is also disturbed because of my illness. For last two months she has not slept properly at night. I found that she was feeling difficulty in speaking." I said, "Now I am leaving, you need rest, I will keep coming to you". She tried to speak, "Nandita is coming today", "It's good that you have called her, she will relieve Gonu and above all, Nandita herself will be happy. She was unnecessarily vexed by reports of your illness, as she is a doctor and for daughter, it's difficult to see mother in pain". "In

America she is also surrounded by her patients, she is very much liked by her patients".

I took the hint; I guessed Nandita didn't treat her patient only with medicine. Her soothing words also, lessened their sufferings. If doctors speak sweet words and have patience to hear, half the disease is cured. Inspite of my request not to talk much, Raj Kumari Ji went on describing the miracles performed by her daughter Nandita by her words and medical treatment. There was happiness on her face, I left her there. I was busy but every second or third day I visited Raj Kumari Ji. One day Nandita brought some soup for her mother. She said, "You leave it", "Call Gonu she will help me, in the mean time you telephone doctor Chawla". Suddenly her hand shook and soup fell down on her mother's body, I was surprised, how a doctor like Nandita could commit such a mistake. Nandita cleared the cloth of her mother and sent Gonu with the soup. Raj Kumari Ji also expressed her anguish, "Gonu, what happened to her sister, why she is absent minded these days? One day Nandita said, "Ma should I sponge your body", Raj Kumari Ji said, " You being a big doctor is not required to do sponge, maid will do or when Gonu returns from school, she will do it". Nandita didn't listen and grip of her finger was loose, thermometer fell down and broke into pieces. When she tried to pick the broken pieces her mother said, leave them, these small jobs don't behove your fingers, I also said, "Yes it's not America. Here you have lots of maid and servants". Nandita gave a mysterious smile, she said, "Your country is also going American way. I also supported her statements, we are importing machines and technology from America but won't it import broken relations and emotions. It is according to Indian tradition that you have left your job and come to India to nurse your mother. Here your mother keeps praising your success as a doctor, there all family relations are breaking".

In the mean time Doctor Chawla arrived and both the doctors started discussing medical problems. I took leave from them. After a few days when I entered the gate, Nandita and Gonu were making their mother for walk in the lawn, Gonu told me, "Aunt, please come here". They made their mother sit there: I went to Raj Kumari Ji and said, "You are looking quiet fresh today. Nandita had cured you. You needed this special doctor to cure you. Gonu tried to speak in protest, I said, "You also serve your mother well, you are a good daughter and doctor, I blessed both". The two daughters were sitting at her feet, like two small children, both of you have served me well, but Nandita is doctor and I have full faith in her knowledge of medicine. Having heard this praise Nandita was overwhelmed, she said, "Please stop, everybody was surprised at her high pitch", "I am tired of being called a doctor, my mother in law, my husband, my son everybody looks at me only as a doctor. I don't serve them only as a doctor, I was anxious and somebody should accept my service as a wife as a daughter and as mother. At least you should accept me and my services as a daughter not as doctor, this hurts me". The warmth of touch of palm, sensitised Raj Kumari Ji's body, new blood was running in her veins, she took her face in her hand and said, "Oh my little baby, your face appears to me as a doctor, I forgot that your are born of me, my darling, please excuse me". How could Gonu tolerate this, she also put her face between her palms; the six eyes came to tears, this was like stream of Ganga, Yamuna and Saraswati. This strange scene made my eyes also wet, and I understood the meaning of falling of the soup from hand of Nandita and the breaking of pieces of thermometer. Everything was clear to me.

□

# 12
# Weapon in a Blunted Hand

Dr Alok Purohit checked his watch while stepping down from the first floor of his house early morning. The thought of reaching a minute late to his office annoyed him. His anger was transferred to his wife, Dr Rekha, she had delayed in preparing breakfast, but next moment he consoled himself. His wife had given up her job to look after the household affairs. Why will she delay in the service of her husband.

Rekha's father had resented the resignation of his daughter from the job. But Rekha had happily accepted the suggestion of her husband. Rekha had no grudge against her situation. The fact was that she was worthily praised by her husband in day to day affairs. According to husband, Dr Rekha had made a great sacrifice, after having high degrees. Giving up job for looking after children was indeed a great sacrifice for educated women. Many times Alok used to express these feeling before his wife.

Rekha didn't like the timidity of her husband. She used to say, "No, I have not made any sacrifice. Hundreds of women look after household duties and they are happy as far as my degree is concerned. It will be useful after sometimes. Dr Alok was impressed with the wisdom of his wife. His thoughts lessened the resentment for delay in breakfast. Before riding his motorcycle, he looked behind. As a successful housewife, Dr Rekha was smiling in farewell to her husband. He started his motorcycle, he saw Mangal running towards him, why should he come here early morning. He knows that it's time for me to go to hospital.

Mangal stood before his motorcycle. Dr Alok saw anger of revenge in his eyes. This was not his ususal way, as he was always humble before him. He used to consider Dr Alok as God. He always said, "who has seen God, may be God is like you". Dr Alok didn't like his flattering words. He would offer him a few rupees and he would go away. Dr Alok started his motor cycle again, "Go away I am getting late". Mangal left his way and said, "You are going to hospital will see you there, I have come to tell you, please fix a pistol in a ring allow me to use weapon". He believed Dr Alok would not deny him. Dr Alok patted his shoulder and said, "You come here at evening. Your madness can't be treated in the hospital, I will treat you here". "Ok I will come in the evening". Dr Alok started his motorcycle and Mangal raised his hand in salutation. Dr Rekha saw him from her house,

Dr Alok used to meet him in the ground of his house. Dr Alok remembered how he met Mangal for the first time, he had a strong body. Dr Alok was angry to find him begging, sometimes he used to put some money on his fingerless palm. One day, he took out his another hand from his pocket and surprised Dr Alok. Both the hand have no fingers and half palm, he asked, "Are you like this by birth"? "No sir". I had palms in both the hands and five fingers in each. They could wield pen or spade. "Ok, ok", please listen to me more. But he had no time. One day he offered him two rupee and said, "Why don't you clean your teeth? It has gone pale. He showed his blunted hands but this could not invoke sympathy in Dr Alok. With this you take your food, you beg, you clean your mouth. Mangal said, "Sir, I earn by begging and my wife feeds me with her hand. I can't brush my teeth", Dr Alok did not say anything and he left him there. While siting in his chair in the hospital, his inventive mind started thinking. He had composed some poems and made some telefilms. He was crazy about social work.

One day an idea came to him, he framed a plastic ring and made a small hole in it. This could hold a tooth brush and Mangal could brush his teeth. This idea filled Dr Alok with happiness. His compounder came to tell him, "sir a beggar has come to see you, his name his Mangal". Dr said "Call him in". When Mangal came he said, "Show me your hand" and he started examining his hand. Mangal laughed and said, "Sir you are dentist, what will you do with my hand".

"Yes I have to treat your teeth but with your hand. I have to take measurement of your hand".

Dr Alok took the measurement of his hand, Mangal didn't forget going to begging and left the doctor thinking. Dr Alok was very happy. He consulted his friend Dr Pama. In two days the plastic ring was ready. Dr Pama was impatiently waiting for Mangal. He searched for Mangal but he was nowhere to be found. Dr Alok was also very anxious but one day suddenly, Mangal appeared. Dr Alok with a tooth paste and brush came down from his house. Mangal had hidden his hands in the blanket. Dr Alok said, "Take out your hand", Mangal smiled and said, "Sir first show me your hand, ultimately Dr Mangal surrendered and he put on the ring in the right hand of Mangal. The ring was properly set and he asked "Does it hurt you"? "No sir". Dr Alok explained look, here is a hole, the brush will fit into it and you can brush your teeth. Dr Alok fixed the brush and applied paste and asked Mangal to brush your teeth. Rekha was looking at the scene with her children and children were also happy. Akshat said, "Dad will ask for water", "Yes I know, yesterday I took out a mug from bathroom. You may take water in that and hand over the mug to him. Dr Alok shouted for Rekha to send something for breakfast. Mangal said, "No sir my belly is full". Dr Alok served him biscuit and tea, Dr Alok said it's not necessary to wear this ring forever, you wear it when you brush your teeth. Dr Rekha shouted from the balcony. "Are you not going to the hospital today? Dr Alok was reminded of the time, he quickly ran up to the house, entered the bathroom. He was thrilled for the good work he had done. After Dr Alok had gone to hospital and children to school, Dr Rekha started thinking, "Dr Alok had gone mad, and it's good to do social work but not at the cost of profession. I want money for my children and household work. He may earn more money but he has no interest in it".

Next morning Mangal came to inform that, he had brushed his teeth properly, Rekha came out. Dr is taking bath, you may go and come tomorrow. Mangal said, kindly tell him that "I have brushed my teeth". "All right go and keep brushing your teeth" Rekha reported to Dr Alok, "Your Mangal had come to tell that he has brushed his teeth." Dr was very happy, did he say anything more, "No", "You may not have asked him", "What should I ask, why should I talk to a beggar?" Her voice was so loud that children gathered there. Doctor didn't speak anything and went to the hospital. After sometime, Mangal came to him and said, "Sir please fix a spoon, so that I can feed myself with my own hand. Why? Does your wife don't feed you now? Has your income increased?" "Yes my income has increase, now I sit for begging in NRI colony. "Sometimes they give five dollars. I learned from them, one dollar is equivalent to rupees fifty". Stop telling why your wife does not feed you. She says since I started brushing my teeth I eat more and she is tied of feeding you. Mangal was in dream land. Dr Alok smiled and he stared his car. In a few days a spoon was fixed in his ring. Dr Alok expected him to come next day but fifteen days lapsed. Dr Alok was busy in his work. One day, he went to Shiv temple, with Rekha. He found Mangal sitting with his wife in the group of beggars. He said, "She is my wife, she burnt her right hand at the time of cooking. I asked her to beg for sometime but I have brought her by force. One person gave him hundred rupees but she didn't stretch her hand to receive it. After sometime Mangal asked his wife, "Please touch the feet". They are Shiv and Parvati for me. Tell me whether you eat with the spoon. What a fool I am, I forget to tell you, Mala burnt her right hand, first I feed her then I eat. You are God for me sir, may your children prosper. After sometime Mangal came to him and said, "Sir! before God one becomes greedy, he asks for marriage, then son and daughter, then money, then education for children and their employment." "What's this? you talk like a philosopher?" "In course of begging one becomes a philopsher sir", "what do you want to say? Do the brush and spoon doesn't work properly?" "No sir! they work properly but I want to tell you, fix a pen also in this ring. Are you educated?", "yes sir! I have passed ninth class, my both hands were lost, so I could not sit for the matriculation exanimation and after sometime my parents died". If I fix a pen, will you write poems? A pen was fixed in his ring, Mangal wrote first word was OM, then Doctor sahib and then God. His wife was overwhelmed to see his letters. After some exercise he wrote, a poem, "Sitting before this temple, I think when the crowd of devotee will scatter and God will be left alone. He will come here, I will touch his feet and make my life, glorious. God met me one day in the guise of man, I was write each line of the poem separately overwhelmed". A Journalist has a wonderful eye for writing. The poem was published in a paper, along with his photo, his brush, spoon and pen in the ring. Now large number of journalist, photographer reached Dr Alok's home. Dr Rekha found her husband more loving that day. The doctor's photo also appeared with Mangal and electronic media highlighted the issue.

Now the people in town organised felicitation for Dr Alok. Mangal was not visible. Rekha said, "Now he will not come, he will write poems, stories and novels", "Yes, he will do that. One day he was saying a beggar knows more about human being and he can write good stories. He was destined to become a story writer, not a beggar. I was just a catalyst". Time went on and many interviews of Dr Alok were published. One morning suddenly Mangal appeared. He was greatly agitated and seemed to be completely changed. What made him seek for weapon? Perhaps somebody might have teased his wife. His wife was beautiful to look at. Dr Alok reached his house. Mangal was standing near his flat, Dr Alok came to him and asked, "What happened? Why are you angry? Will you go for dacoity or kill someone with the money you get in begging?" "Yes, I will kill the man who is inciting me against you". He poses as your friend, he says that because of me you have become famous. In newspaper, your name and photographs were published, he asked me to get silver ring from you and talked dirty about you and jealous of you. I won't leave him alive. Dr Alok put his hand on his shoulder and said, "Have you heard the name of Tulisdas?", "I read Ramcharitmanas every day, Ram killed Ravan and Balli, he kept killing rogue in the forest. He is our God, yes it's alright but Tulisdas has written about bad people. For them miss fortunate of others is their fortune. They are happy, when somebody is destroyed".

It's all right, there was a seminar when I was in eighth class. "Which is superior? sword or pen?" I had spoken in favour of pen and quoted, Tulsidas, Kabir and Rahim and other poets. But now it's time to take sword against the culprit. "Sir, please expand this hole and fix a pistol in it". "Go away, return my ring, you don't need a brush, a spoon and a pen. Because of your violence, God has taken your hands". Doctor's voice was so loud that large number of people gathered there. Mangal fell on the feet of the Doctor and said, "Pardon me sir, I forgot the couplet regarding sandal and serpent. Bad association does not affect man of good character as sandal is not affected by a poisonous snake". Doctor Alok started going to his house and his wife said, "Listen to him properly and the doctor came to Mangal and his eyes were saying, "pen is a mighty instrument, keep it holding."

□

# 13

# When Chaos Prevails

There was a time when Haripad used to look at the bpdig buildings of the town from a distance. The house of his employer sent him to dreamland. "A time may come when he would have a pukka room for himself with a door and window and when you return home in the evening Sunayana waiting for you. He would wave hand from a distance and having reached home, he would close the door both of them would dream of the future.

But one room will not be enough, he will have many children. Though he had no parents. After his birth, mother died and his father left him when he was within teens. He inherited the employment office after death of his father. The small cottage and the government service; these were his assets. He had no one in this world; he liked the crowded house of his friend, Patiram. After his duty hours, he would be attracted to the house of his friend. From that family, he brought a person which made his house a home. Hopes started sprouting and he told Sunayana, he wanted many kids but gradually he realised that

Sunayana did not like children much and one day she said, "If you want many kids, you can marry another woman. I will give birth to only one child". One day Sunayana informed him, she was on a family way. He couldn't hold himself and said, "I want four children at a time. "No, No", she said "I don't want to die". You want children not me. When he reached his employers house, he said, "Memsahib, my wife is on a family way". "Take her to hospital to consult a doctor". He had no patience, He brought his wife Suanyana to memsahib. She was surprised to see such a beautiful woman. "O! your wife is so beautiful, she is so fair and you a dark one". In the hospital the nurse and doctors also said the same thing. He was happy with his wife and looked after her but gradually the town was under the spell. He didn't understand anything, he used to go to a teacher who was a great help to him. Haripad went to him. He heard a voice coming from inside, "Did you not feel ashamed? At the age of 50 you got vasectomy done. Now you have a daughter in law in your house, I feel shame in talking". "I didn't have any choice, you live in the house and don't know what is happening outside. Teachers and Government servants are tortured. If one is in Government service, one has to suffer these humiliations". Haripad heard this but he could not understand anything, He called Mater sahib, "Who Haripad come in". He was surprised to see Master Sahib, "What has happened to you sir". "See and hear, don't speak its Government order, don't print, don't read and don't speak". I don't understand anything,

"Don't try to understand, why it's happening so, it's should not happen. Master Sahib took a deep breath and said, "There is no question of any ones likes or dislikes. Keep suffering and following the orders, freedom is in danger. Haripad could not understand anything but he realised predicament. When he came back home, he was informed that for a paltry sum of money, Patiram had also got his operation done. Haripad was in precarious situation. In the hospital, he use to protest against vasectomy but he was a government servant. One day he took courage and pleaded with his memsahib, "Memsahib, please stop your husband, he should not force people to undergo vasectomy, after all it is natural right to have children". "Keep quiet, now a days you speak much. Limit yourself to hospital work". Haripad kept silence. They could not sleep and he kept thinking how to stop this. He had no power to stop the orders coming from Delhi. Everyday doctors would be happy to see the increasing number of vasectomy in the hospital. It caused him tension and he suffered from hernia. Mamsahib took him to hospital and he did not know that his vasectomy was also done. He was informed that your vasectomy has been done. Gradually it came to light that his Patiram has got his vasectomy done because his salary was stopped. His wife was also sad. Out of the sadness, a protest rose in his mind. He left going to the hospital. One day he took up a stone and threw on a civil surgeon and he ran away. Police started looking for him. He hid behind the statue of Khudiram Bose and didn't go home. News came to

Patiram that Haripad has left his house in fear of police. Sunaina can't live alone, she came to her brother Patiram's house. Patiram said, "Sunaina you don't come to my house. Haripad is against the government. They may put me also in jail. Sunayan started crying loudly. Now police was searching Haripad. They had warrant of arrest against him. Many times, he came early morning to console his wife Suanayan. She was on a family way. News of arrest of leaders and lathi charges against public demonstrations were pouring in. Sunayana told her husband, "My brother has closed the door of the house for me. You are absconding, were will I go"? At the time for delivery, he called his nani for looking after his wife. Police came searching for him, but they could not find him. They took some items of the house, nani shouted for help, but no one came. She kept shouting at the police and government.

Now she told Sunayana, "Let us go to my house. She delivered the child at Sunayana's house. She used to console Sunayana, "Haripad's nana was absconding like him. Those of the days of English under the leadership of Gandhi, he was fighting against the British, He threw bomb on a white man. He was caught and sent to jail. Hripad's mother was born while he was in jail. He didn't see the face of his child". "Was he not released from the jail?" Nani concealed the fact of hanging of her husband; she said "Have patience. Haripad will be released, now there is no English rule. It is government of Gandhi people". Patiram informed I that now he was a father. His wife had delivered a son. Having heard the news, Haripad ran to his nani's house. Sunayana was in deep sleep and the child was sleeping in her lap. His nani was sitting at the gate. She said, "Don't go inside, mother and child have just slept". But he did not listen to her and took the child in his lap. Child was only 24 hours old and Haripad left his kisses on him. Suddenly the police jeep came and headlight of police jeep spread around the cottage. Sunayana woke up, the police inspector asked his men to surround the cottage; he was hand cuffed. "Come to jail", neighbours got up but they didn't have the courage to come to his house. He guessed Patiram might have informed the police. He passed by the statute of Khudiram Bose and bowed to it. The torcher in the jail did not affect him, but memory of Sunayana and small child used to make him restless. Now he was weak and suffered from several diseases in the jail. Once Sunayana came to see him in the jail; she could not recognise him. Now his hair were grey, he had long beard and Sunayana did not tell him about the death of his child. After six month, suddenly a change came, many leaders and their supporters were freed from jail but Haripad was booked under heinous offence. Talks of elections loomed everywhere. Sunayana was angry; she used to take part in election rallies. She used to meet with some people who were earlier in jail. She used to ask, when her husband would return. They all used to console her. "Let us form a new Government and he will be released." She had a busy schedule; she would put herself in every election rally. She was presented as symbol of being tortured. On the day of voting, long lines were approaching the booths. Sunanyana could not keep standing for long, she fell down. The workers helped her. Patiram came to her, what has happened to you. This Government has done much heinous crime. Now you come to my house, Haripad will come home. New government will be formed. Sunayana could not bear his word any more. "Go away, don't touch me. I am dead for you". She was almost life less, somebody informed Haripad will be released in a day or two as counting has been started and results will be in the favour of a new Government. At the dead of night, she suddenly woke up and started shouting and running, "let me come, let me come", People followed her, she was shouting and running, "I am coming, I am coming". People followed her tried to stop her. She reached the house of civil surgeon. She took a stone and threw at the window. The glass was broken to pieces. The sound of the broken glasses shook the foundation of Saafardung Kothi in Delhi. She was tired of throwing stone and soon her body almost became lifeless. They brought her body to the house. The whole town was celebrating the victory at the dead of night. She was left alone in the house. Next day new Government was formed, a policeman came to Haripad barrack and said, "Government has released you from the jail, you may go out now", but Haripad was no more. The doctor examined both death bodies and he said both died at the same time. Now they will meet in next birth. They will dream, whether dream is realized or not, no one can prevent you from dreaming.

□

# 14
# The Pickle Earthen Pot

For every mother, all her children are equal and every child has equal share in her love it cannot biased. Sometime or the other every child either feels that he is favourite of his mother or feels being deprived of mother's love.

My mother died 20 years ago. Even after her death she is alive in us. Her laughter, tears, anger and separation everything is vivid. It is reflected in our laughter and tears. It affects our emotions and sometimes restricts it. For my mother, her domestic utensils were as much important as her children. With the same care, she used to look after them as she used to look after her sons and daughter. So those who closely observed her had same regard for her utensils as well as for her children. The servants were also conscious of this strength and weakness of my mother. If any of her utensils was damaged, the person responsible for it was prepared for punishment. With great care, she would cut raw vegetables and arrange them. Her expectation was that the person who washes and cooks them should take the same care. Even the burning fuel had to be according to her standard. Dry sticks would forget its nature and burn according to the control of my mother in medium flame so that she could prepare food according to the taste of her husband and children. Her empire was limited to the kitchen and its care. She didn't find time to listen to rumours and stories of the neighbourhood or go on pilgrimage or marketing. She found great pleasure in preparing tasty food and serve with love to her husband and children and got satisfaction from that. If any day the taste of her food was not up to her expectation, she could know it from the colour of the food. She would not serve the food to anybody that day and she would get to bed on the pretext of headache. For her, preparing food was a sacred ritual. Behind every art, there is sacred ritual, why not the same for art of cooking? She used different prefix to address her husband. And these would change according to the colour of her face like a rainbow. For outsiders, he was master sahib, for children he was babuji and for servants he was maalik. But the best words she has for him was *khanihar*(one who eats). Perhaps in the sixty years of marital life, she had never taken food without serving her husband. Whether it is as late as 2pm in the day or 12 in the night, she would take food only after serving her husband and generally in the same plate. During the summer, she would sit before him and wielding hand fan to her husband and would ask him, taste of the each food items. Not only that she would ask about every item of the food without that she had no satisfaction. She used to observe every bite he used to take, to feed any anybody was a sacred ritual for her. Nobody could disturb her in this sacred ritual. She wouldn't tolerate any body trying to disturb her at that time. A disturbed one had to be prepared for punishment, whether a servant or neighbour or even children. On this pretext she would scold them, "were you missing the train? Why did you shout? Didn't you see that I was feeding my husband".

On that day also, mother was in total concentration in feeding her husband, suddenly he asked for pickle, mother was wielding hand fan. If she would go to bring the pickle, she feared her husband would face heat and precipitation. Because of pain in her waist, she would take more time so she called "Madhu go and bring some pickle, it is placed in wooden alamirah in the old black mud pot", I also showed promptness in serving it. She was telling, "New pickle is not prepared for use, I have not oiled it, I am tired of asking oilman to come, if he comes, I will take care of him. Suddenly sound of falling mud pot was heard. "The pickle mud pot fell on me and whole oil poured on me and it went into pieces". Before I could speak anything my mother heard the sound of falling of pot and it turning into pieces. Mother didn't come to me; the last cry of the mud pot kept piercing her ears. For two days, she laid on bed, many people came to console her, "it was just a mud pot, a new will come, look at your daughter, she is crying incessantly and that could have bad effect on her health". But mother did not get up nor did she look at me, I could not feel if she would shout at me or beat me but her silence was more eloquently hurting me. My aunt knew the history of every stage of the life of the mud pot. In supporting my mother's sorrow on the demise of the mud pot, she told me, "she had called the potter and requested him, giving the details of the pot she required, size and shape and circumference and height was described in details. The potter listened with great attention, he with great care prepared the pot and when my sister saw it she refused to accept it, "Look how thick is the neck and look at the bottom it will tumble. I don't want this red colour, I want this black colour, I don't want pot for water, it is for pickles, it will get stronger after it consumes oil for many years. It will continue for my life and after me, my daughter-in-law will also use it." The potter made many trials but she didn't accept anyone. One day he said, "Madam you come to my house and find for yourself, nobody can say what will come out of a potters fire place and women's womb, from one fire place different types of pot come out, some distorted and someone eyed, or some fat or thin. Children born of same womb are different, even twins are different, you may find some mud pot of your choice, please come to my house. For sometimes she kept thinking about the philosophy of the potter and one day she went to the potter's house and she picked up her choice. For two days, she kept preparing the pot of her choice for the final work, she put pickle and oil in it and with a thin cloth muzzled its mouth. She did not allow anybody to touch this; nobody could touch it with dirty hand or unwashed hand and mouth. She should not be in menstruation period or without bath. She would herself take out pickle from the pot. Her pot would continue for years and she was suffering from pain in the waist, she could not rise to bring pickle for her husband. She called her daughter. Today's children have no patience. Although she is her own daughter, she does not have the patience of her mother".

As if she was telling the story of not a mud pot but one of her children as an effort to console her she said, *"let by gones be by gones*, now look after your daughter". But mother was not prepared to forget, I realised for the first time that she loved anything else more than me, this hurt me very much somewhere deep inside. My father used to read loudly the second chapter of Hindi version of the Gita. His aim was to send the message to my mother but her empire didn't allow the penetration of detachment. My father believed that one day she would listen to the message of the Gita.

Sometimes mother used to be detached, sometimes she was dejected at the ignoring of her emotions by her husband. On the destruction of the pot, this detachment was obvious; not looking at her beloved daughter was an expression of detachment. In that house the end of the pickle pot was end of a generation. Now instead of mud pot the pickles were preserved in big glass jars.

Mother's days were numbered, she would sit in her cot and call others from there, gradually she became silent and the silence turned into eternal silence. Everybody was crying, she was decorated as a married woman for the last time. Her granddaughter decorated her in a red sari, a big red bindi on the forehead and a deep line of red vermilion between her white hairs. Her feet were painted red, my father burst into tears when he saw her. All his knowledge of Gita, were blown to pieces. Looking at his, love for the dead body of his wife, tears came to the eyes of everyone present there. "I was sitting at a distance, *Chachi* came to me and said, come and meet your mother, pay obeyance to her, now you will not get your mother back. Are you still angry with your mother, for your mother there was no difference between the mud pot and her child".

She took me to my mother, I gathered courage, I started to read her face, which had no emotions. There was detachment; this was the same silence which she had assumed on the demise of the mud pot. For last fifteen years I could not define the silence but her silence was eloquent. She was a *yogini*, a very pious soul for whom there was no difference between a pickle pot and a child. I understood the philosophy of her life, I went to my father and recited the line of Gita, " As people discard old cloth and assume new". My father's hiccups made me silent. Perhaps, it was not my mother's body but a broken mud pot. He looked at the decorative body of my mother and asked me, "Go bring the Gita, I will make her hear in detail; she has been escaping from it. Always engaged in household works, now she has to listen, where will she go"? All her family stared weeping loudly, I was also part of the tribe.

□

# 15

# Unnamed Relationship

Scanning the invitation letter in her hand, Chitra ji was weighing the inner significance of the letter, she read it again. The guests gathered on the marriage occassion will ask, "who am I and what my relation with Shaligram Ji. What answer Shaligram Ji will give, I never thought of the relations formed between us".

The truth is that, she never understood what this relationship was, she never recalled Shalimgram Ji. It was Shaligram ji who took initiative to remember the relation. After long deliberation, Chitra Ji decided to go to Bhopal. She had to travel long distance by bus and train and that too in summer season. Shaligram Ji had assured her on telephone that she would not face any difficulty, I have arranged for accommodation according to the season. I think our guests will have no difficulty and you are a special guest, Chitra Ji didn't have any reply. She decided to go and forgot about the difficulties. She took her seat in a Volvo bus service. Her mobile rang, it was from Shaligram Ji, he said, "when your bus will reach Delhi bus stand,

Rakesh will meet you. He has your rail ticket with him". She did not say anything, not even this that she had already purchased the rail ticket. The moment the bus stopped in Delhi, Rakesh came searching for her. He took her luggage and said, "If you have a rail ticket, kindly give it to me, I will get it cancelled. This is AC second class ticket for you. The train will depart from Nizamuddin station in the evening. I am coming with you". Chitra ji handed over the sleeper class ticket to him, she took a three wheeler from Gol market to her friend's quarter. In the evening everything happened as Rakesh had said. Early morning the train reached Bhopal junction and a young man came to her and touched her feet. He said, "I am Deepak, son of Shaligram Kashyap". Chitra Ji, blessed him and followed, road was crowded. Sometimes the car had to blow horn but there was perfect silence inside. Chitra Ji wanted to talk to the young man, she didn't know anything about the town. She was going to ask about Bhopal. Suddenly Deepak said, "Should I call you aunt, the marriage party will come in the evening. It is local affair, so it will be timely. I have heard that you are returning tomorrow, you don't have much time. My father said you are coming to Bhopal for the first time. Naturally you would like to see Bhopal, it's a beautiful city. My cousin will take you to see Bhopal", she nodded her head. She expressed her gratitude to the person who arranged all these things. She could have expressed thanks to the young man but said nothing, Deepak said, "father has great appreciation for you. He says you are an incarnation of Goddess. Don't know why you didn't come to see Bhopal and never invited us to Shimla. Had great desire to see you, so leaving behind many works I came to see you". Before Chitra Ji could speak anything, the driver had stopped the car, near the guest house. Deepak took the luggage and followed her inside the room. He spoke, "Just get fresh, will have breakfast at home and then will go to see Bhopal, the lunch is also planned at home, Marriage is in the evening". Chitra Ji didn't speak anything, after bidding fare well to him, Chitra Ji came to the room and bolted it and sat on the bed. "Deepak is a good boy, around 20 and sincere. He has a great respect for his father, people are unnecessarily worried that new generation is deviating. This young man had a place in my heart but for this the credit should goes to his father she thought". When she got fresh, Naresh came to her, he invited her to breakfast. "You are aunt of Deepak, I am his friend. I have met his two aunts but I am seeing you for the first time". Shaligram Ji reached the gate quickly, he welcomed Chitra Ji. I took her to view Bhopal and she liked three lakes. Perhaps Chitra Ji could not have recognised the man, standing before her, she folded her hands and reciprocated with a smile.

Breakfast was arranged in his verandah. Some people were still having breakfast, and when Shaligram Ji took Chitra Ji to the table, the guest became anxious to know about her. We never saw her earlier, nobody had an answer. Shaligram Ji's wife

Mala also came, "Mala Ji" someone asked "Who is she, a beautiful women in Kota sari". Mala Ji looked around, another woman asked in sub dued voice, "For which Shaligram Ji is serving the plate with his own hand". They were right; Mala Ji saw her husband was standing before Chitra Ji with a cup of tea for her. A cultured lady of almost of her age, taking breakfast, Shaligram Ji never mentioned about her. She had read the list of invitees, but could not find Chitra Ji's name. There were many questions, but it was not the proper time to ask. At the time of rituals, everybody kept asking about this women, she came for the lunch. One of sister-in-laws of Shaligram Ji, asked Chitra Ji, "Where have you come from"? Another sister in law wanted to know as to how she knew Shaligram ji. In the meantime Shaligram himself appeared and directed his sister-in-law to serve other guest.

While resting in the guest house, remembered the incident of 25 years ago. Husband wife and two kids were going to Manali from Shimla. After sometime, the car fell in a gorge, the husband's head was severely injured. No chance of his gaining consciousness, her talks with doctor and doctor proposal before her to take a quick decision. Chitra Ji standing alone and two children beside her, no relatives were near her. She had to deicide, everything was gone, and she was requested to give whatever was saved. With her offer, a person on death bed was to live. Every scene was alive in her memory. She decided not to remember them on this, auspicious occassion. Gone is gone, she on the occassion of his daughter daughter's marriage she wanted to think of auspicious things. This was the demand of the occassion. The marriage party came, men and women gathered. They were haunted by this question – what is the relation with Shaligram Ji. He introduced Chitra Ji to his brother in law (samdhi) on the door. But he didn't introduce to him, his sister-in-law and their husband. This news quickly pervaded the atmosphere. After dinner, the rituals of marriage started, Shaligram Ji was called by the pandit for offering his daughter to marriage. Before sitting on the mandap, he was searching for Chitra Ji. His sister-in-law pointed towards Chitra ji. His wife Mala also noticed this, and said angrily, "Now sit down and concentrate on rituals. Shaligram Ji spoke in loud voice", "Chitra Ji please come in the mandap, my daughter deserves your blessings". Chitra Ji was touched from inside. She stood up and said, "You proceed for the rituals and offer your daughter to the groom, I am a widow. Society does not permit a widow to come in the mandap. I wish your daughter the very best and that is why I am sitting at a distance, you fulfil your duty", saying this she sat down. "I don't believe in these customs for my family, nobody is more auspicious than you. Without your kindness, neither I nor would my family be alive. Please come and offer kanyadan". The pundit was also worried and said, "Your guest is correct and call your wife with you for Kanyadan. Only non widow sit in the mandap". Shaligram Ji spoke loudly, "All of you are anxious to know about Chitra Ji. Now I have to reveal her identity, without that your attention will be diverted. Now you listen, twenty five years ago her husband was seriously injured in an accident. His brain was dead, his body was brought to the hospital in which I was also hospitalized, my heart was almost non functional. The Surgeon decided if a live, heart can be available for transplantation, I could be saved. We have heard of eye donation, kidney donation but heart donation is possible only when heart is alive. Nobody will donate the heart of a living one, Chitra Ji husband's heart was alive, and his brain was dead. Dr Sharma requested her, "We cannot save your husband, but if you agree his heart can be transplanted to the other, that person will survive." What impact this advice had on Chitra Ji, I don't know, Chitra Ji gave permission. The heart in my body is the heart of her husband. In last twenty years, she never mentioned, never she saw me, I also didn't know her. She didn't try to search for me, I was very worried, and I couldn't express my gratitude to the donor. Two years back, I went to Shimla and saw D. Sharma, I could not meet her. Dr Sharma gave her mobile number. On calling, I revealed her identity and sent an invitation to her. She had faced many difficulties in life but still she agreed to attend the marriage of my daughter. For the first time, I saw her this morning. Now tell me who is more auspicious to my family than this lady. My marriage and children is because of her, I owe everything to her". Mala stood up from the mandap, she came to Chitra and touched her feet and dragged her to the mandap. A group of ladies wiped their tears and blessed the couple. There is no need in a name for a relationship. There a many relations in the courtyard but the relation between Shaligram Ji and Chitra Ji was unique and it could not be named.

□

# 16

# The Light Festival of a Lamp

Ganesh was invincible. He was born in a small village of Madhubani district of ten huts. His bro-in-law brought him to the town, He was about sixteen year old, this is my surmise. Even his mother didn't know the date, month and year of his birth, so why should the son remember his birthday. He didn't have to celebrate his birthday and increase a number of candles every year. My son asked him, "Ganesh how old are you? He replied, "I am about ten year old". "Do don't lie, your moustache is coming up and you say only ten". He was sad and came to me, "Mom I am ten year old, ha-ha you are only nine, go and do your work. Put water in the pot and do dusting". He was happy and engaged in his work, I was the only person to support him in the house. It was hardly six months, he was with us, when his brother-in-law brought him to me. He didn't know how to behave. Usually he used to stand out in the balcony and look in the sky or in the park, full of plants. I didn't know what he used to think. "What are you doing Ganesh"?

He would get startled, whatever tool he had in the hand, he would start using it. Sometimes, he would be lost in the midst of scrapping the floor. "Ganesh are you sleeping?", then his hand would start working. For a month, the inmates of my house would worry. When rainy season came, Ganesh became vocal. Every day he would speak two to four words and entering the second month, he could speak, five hundred words. Then my son scolded him, "what is this you are chatting always?" He would shake his head and say, "I am not chatting I was saying". His statements were not like short scene of the television, they were like folk serials. It came to my understanding that in six months, he has not forgotten his village farm, cottage and his mother even for a moment. He had no inferiority complex for his village and its atmosphere.

One day with a great care I prepared sweet porridge and asked him, "Ganesh did you take it and how did you like it?" Perhaps it was for the first time that he had tasted porridges of four litre milk with 100gms rice and dry fruits. Instead of appreciating my porridges, he would appreciate porridge prepared by his mother with quarter of milk, half a kilo of rice, two litres of water. "My mother also used to prepare sweet porridge, it was very sweet. I used to take it with my father, one full plate. On the day of holi festival, mother gave me full plate porridge".

His mom might have prepared porridge on the Holi day, but porridge prepared by me and that of his mother were much different in colour and taste. But

Ganesh didn't appreciate my porridge, I gave him in a small pot, four spoons full of porridge and his mother used to feed him his belly full.

He used to have the same comments about other food items prepared in his house. In the kitchen whenever preparations of gram powder, maize chapatti, suji halwa, his comment would begin. "My mother also used to prepare" and his endless story would start. Surely there was a great difference between his small hut in the village and my three rooms flat in Delhi. While wiping the floor of my house, he would remember his mother wiping his hut with cow dung. "He never belittled himself. It didn't matter for me. Children like Ganesh's appreciation of his mother was soothing to me. But he could not tolerate t twelve year old son and always used to fight with him. My son used English to demoralize him & his language was Maithili mixed Hindi. Ganesh would make faces at my son & tried to have shield from my mother. This made us laugh, He got numb, but there was no trace of defeat on his face. There was no shame on his face, He was unable to make us understand what he wanted. I stopped laughing and said, "Does your mother also speak English"?

There was loud laughter among the audience but Ganesh could not laugh. For the first time he was serious and remained serious till evening. I asked Ganesh, "what is this?" and he didn't reply and went to the balcony. I followed him and stood before him, he was looking to the sky. Two drops of tears trickled down his cheeks, for some time at least. I said to him, "Ganesh are you missing your mother"? This consoled him. And showing his shining teeth he said, "My mother did not speak English". My mother said, "Learn English then only you can stay in Delhi". I was looking for learning English from Bhaiya ji.

"Good-good you have started learning Hindi and then English will be taught. Now go to the milk booth for milk and collect the clothes". My soft words made him relax and I was happy that he happily entered the kitchen to fetch the milk pot. During the festive season of Dusheera, he saw Durga puja and Ram leela and he was reminded of Navrattra mela. He remembered how his mother would go to mela wearing new sari and purchase balloons of twenty paisa for him and some sugar candy for one rupee. He would describe his mother's bindiya and slippers. Now it was time for Diwali night. My house was being painted and on the other hand, Ganesh's broadcast started elucidating his mother style of cleaning the house. I was apprehensive he would belittle the grand Delhi Diwali as compared, to his village Diwali, I was waiting for the time. Couple of days earlier in Delhi, crackers firing of had started. In couple of minutes he came running to me and asked, "What is this loud sound? "Diwali is coming up, children are lighting the crackers". Why two days earlier?" I avoided discussion with him, "In Delhi, every day is Diwali, go do your work." "Hey mummy, my mother would also wash her tin box. In that box, my mother keeps new sari and some other clothes". "Stop! I know your mother has a box and good sari and other clothes. There is everything in your house. Now go clean, my four Godrej almirahs. All these Almirahs and utensils of bronze, steel are still to be cleaned". I used to help him in cleaning these things but he was not to be cowed down by my hundreds of utensils and I had no time to revise his memory. He would start telling about his mother's celebrating Diwali. "Stop now, first let Diwali be over and then I will listen to your mother's stories of Diwali". But he didn't stop, while preparing sweets in the kitchen, decorating floor and preparing for lighting lamp, I always used to ask him to keep quiet, but he would not listen. After 10 at night, he stopped talking, in spite of my son's request, he didn't go to burst crackers and fire candles. He was not moved by the request. He went in the corner of the roof and stood there, kept listening to the sound of the crackers. In the morning he got up late, I called for him but he didn't turn up. I went upstairs and found him sleeping in a corner, "were you awake for the whole night? Are you tired", He looked like my spent mud lamp. He looked like the ruminants of burnt crackers and candle fires. I could see his face and brought him down, while taking tea I asked him Ganesh, "Now tell me about Diwali of your mother". He was silent, his head was down, I was surprised to find him silent even mentioning of his mother. Suddenly he started speaking like an empty tank. "My mother.... also .... used to ....keep...one mud lamp..... in Delhi crore of rupees are spent in the celebrations of Diwali. In comparison to this house, how small was his mother's Diwali", But he was neither astonished nor sad. I was sad at his situation, apprehensive of his mother looking smaller in front of mummy. I never wanted his mother to be defeated by mummy, Ganesh mother was his mother and she was invincible. What if she has only one mud lamp for Diwali.

□

# 17
# A Household Sannyasi

Kanaklata's repeated request didn't have any effect on her husband she called Hari Kishorji. Hari Kishor Ji gave many examples of the rigid attitude of her husband but then consoled her. "For you I will talk to him, I think now both of you should live with your son, He needs you. And tomorrow you will need him, after all old age cannot be spent without the help of children. During youth, trees are planted so that, in old days, you may spend time under the shadow of that tree. Take my example. There was a time when everybody danced on my tune but today I have to behave as per my son's suggestions and directions. One has to transfer the rights of management of house. One becomes vanprasthi, one who accepts this remains happy", She said. "Dear brother I understand this", Hari Kishore Ji assured her that he would talk to her husband soon". "But where is he, for last some days a sannyasi from Haridwar had come, he is in his attendance. My daughter in law has sent three letters from Delhi. Yesterday a telegram also came, she is on the family way and it's her eighth month". There was a tension on the face of Kanak Lata. Her desire to attend the birth of new generation of Mohan Babu was crushed under the weight of his obdurate behaviour. Hari Kishore Ji consoled her and said, "I will take some senior people of the village and go to him. If he doesn't listen to me, he will listen to members of the village". Kanak Lata behaved like a child and emotionally urged Hari Kishore Ji, "Please go today itself, if he will agree, we he will go to Delhi by evening train. They are waiting for us, I have prepared everything, I have gathered old mustard oil, honey, Kohl, ajawain, old rice, lentils, I have got some old clothes washed".

Hari Kishore Ji kept looking at her face and watching her impatience, idea flashed in his mind, "Kanak Lata Ji all these items are now old, people living in towns do not use them. Your daughter in law will not allow the child to be massaged with mustard oil. And doctors advice against application of Kohl", But he kept his advice to himself and left the place.

Kanka Lata kept waiting till late night with food for her husband. Mohan Babu woke her up in the easy chair, in which she had slept. "Get up! next morning you have to go to Delhi. After all you organise a panchayat of village people against me". Kanak Lata didn't care for his complaint and arranged for his dinner. She kept arranging things for the journey. In the morning, Hari Kishore Ji and his wife were first to bid farewell to them. "He said, "Don't worry for here, stay in Delhi at peace, help your son and daughter-in-law and get them serve you". Mohan Babu looked at Hari Kishore Ji with a grievance in his eyes. You have deviated me from my path; a few days ago he had revealed his future plan to some of his friends. "After 30 years of service as a teacher, I have retired; retirement is for ending of worldly affairs, I don't want to be tied down to the worldly life. I am a perfect sanatani, one has to spend the four stages of life according to the shastras. Now I have to proceed to Van Prastha. All these household works, children and their problems are ties of Maya. I want to go and spend the rest of my time in some Ashram". For last 30, years he has been telling these things to his wife. After the marriage of Sheela, Rita and son Anil, he had said to his wife, "Now leave this house, you have ten Bighas of land. It is for my son Anil to decide what he will do with that, we will go to Haridwar, and rest of life will be spent in the service of mother Ganges. I don't know why, even in old days people keep entangled in the family problems and lead a life of hell".

For Kanka Lata the advice of her husband was not new but she had no time to think of these things as she was deeply involved in the welfare of the family.

They reached Delhi, their son and daughter-in-law were always in their service. They were always careful about their likes and dislikes. Kanak Lata was highly overwhelmed as if her lifelong desire was fulfilled.

At the time of birth of her own Anil, she could not enjoy happiness of maternity. The complications in looking after the child denied her happiness of maternity. At the time of birth of her grandson, she realised as she has become mother for the first time. Sometimes she would compare the limbs of the new born baby with that of Mohan Babu, sometimes with great grand father-in-law and sometimes with father-in-law. She was overwhelmed with the child in her lap while nursing him, She used to tell the stories of the ancestors but Mohan Babu was like a detached lotus in water. He was un moved and concentrated in himself, he would look at the activity of his wife with a detachment.

After the birth of the grandson, the increasing attachment of his wife Kanak Lata in the household work made him obtuse. Kanka Lata did not care for his words, She was always talking about the grand child, "Look his fingers are exactly like yours and his nose is like your father and his eyes; they resemble Anil. Was not Anil like him 30 years ago? How much your mother suffered in taking care of the child. Her sari never went dry. She never gave Anil to me, but I was the mother only for the sake of breast feeding. It is now that I have become a mother, you never became a father; you never touched your son with your hands, once when your father was playing with Anil. Suddenly Anil addressed you as a 'father'. And you felt so embarrassed.

Mohan Babu was unmoved, neither the services of his son and daughter in law nor with his wife, submerged in happiness of the family life, nor with the daughter in law who used to be very careful about his likes and dislikes. Kanak Lata had trained daughter-in-law about likes and dislikes of Mohan Babu.

One day, the small child relieved himself in her lap, her hands and sari were dirty, she asked her husband Mohan Babu, "Please bring a jug of water, I can't get up, you need help me in washing the child". This was too much for Mohan Babu, "I will not be a slave to a woman's snare, I will leave this house". Kanak Lata kept waiting and the child kept crying. She tried to console the child, wait wait your grand father is bringing water and then you will be washed and a good boy, I will apply talc to you, Dada ji is coming". But dada ji was nowhere to be seen, Siddarth had left his house in youth and he was blessed with Bodhi. Mohan Babu spent three fourth of his life in the family, now he came out after breaking all the shackles. Kanka Lata waited. She used to console her son and daughter in law. He used to tell the family story to her grand child and pray to God for the welfare of her husband. Ultimately she forgot to wait for him and gave up the hope of his return.

Sri Kishore Ji had come to Delhi for some work, he reported, "After you left the village, the share holders have become uncontrolled, they don't listen to me. They had planted wheat in two bighas, the crop is good but they gave only five measures as your share. The mango trees were full of fruits but your man said hardly any fruit has come. Kanak Lata tried to console Hari Kishore ji, my great grandfather had planted the trees, and they are now too old to bear fruits. Kanka Lata said further, "My great father-in-law had planted tree in his house and look that tree has given fruits; I am engaged in looking after it. After he grows a bit, I will go to the village", Hari Kishore was over whelmed. The philosophy of life of Kanak Lata touched his heart, he said, "The world would not have moved without mother and sister like you. Males analysed life but women create life and look after life so they are great. They are unique creations of God, engaged in preserving the creations. Kanka Lata said; "I would request you to go to Haridwar once. May be my husband is in some ashram there, I want to know about his welfare. Anil and his wife are very upset they think they are cause of his leaving the house. The truth is that after the death of my husband's mother, he has become a shareholder in my affection. As long as he was only my husband, I had grievances but now, I pray to God that he should have no mental or physical problems. He is now as good as Anil for me". Kanak Lata started shedding tears, Hari Kishore had read in the shastra about many facets of women's life, now he was having darshan of motherhood's incarnation. In the mean time, the child started bubbling, Baba, Baba he has learnt only this word. Kanak Lata took him up, "Yes your Baba will come and he will take you to the market on his shoulder. He will buy things for you and in old days you will be his support". Hari Kishore Ji asked in a low voice, "I hope you have no difficulty for the whole day looking after child. It might tire you Kanak Lata replied, "You have your grand children, sometimes you should play with them, your time will be spent fruitfully & you will get energy also they are like the incarnation of God. Kaushalya's Krishna does not allow you to be tired, they keep you fresh. Hari Kishor Ji remembered his fast, last year when he was not well, doctor advised him to play with his grand children that would be more effective than medicine.

Time passed on, the child started calling Ma to his Grandmother, he could now walk, now Kanak Lata was haunted by her hereditary property and the house in the village. One day she told her son, Anil, "Now I would like to return to village, I have to look at the things there". "Mother how will you leave alone in the village"? Nobody is alone in the village. The moment I reach there, neighbours will flock to me. People come alone in this world and they go alone, one has to be prepared for this. Anil said, "I think, I take leave for a month and all of us should go to the village, after making arrangements for the land and house, we will come back here. I will go to village every six months, will not leave you alone now". "No for me it is necessary to live in the village for some time, I will come here after every six months". "How will you like without your grandson". "I can live, one has to be free from the snares of life, there are children in the neighbourhood. They may be poor but they are like Gods. They accompany for the whole day, sometimes I give them small chocolates, sometimes tell them stories and when I come to you, they ask me, when I would go back. You needed me I came to your house, now they are waiting for me, let me go; one should go where one is needed and stay there as long as she is not a burden". Anil kept watching the face of his mother and the flow of philosophy of life coming out of her mouth. Her philosophy of life was the philosophy of the Gita, she was not highly educated, never read the Gita and the Upnishad, she only lived the philosophy of great books. Anil said, "Ok, I take leave from office for a week and will go to the village".

With his dusty feet the child came and sat in her lap. For some time she kept playing with him; how she was going to the village. The child didn't understand anything but she kept on telling about her plans to go to her village. She gave him a toy and went to bathroom, he fell from the Sofa, he started crying, but he stopped crying, she wondered and feared the door was open, she quickly came out, the child was not there, she went on calling for him, she could not find him and came out of the house. In the park she found a person in dirty saffron clothes, his hair and beard were grown up, he was playing with the child. Kanak Lata ran to him and shouted who are you, a thief or child abductor. Kanak Lata was surprised, she looked at the eyes of the stranger, things had changed. Mohan Babu could not look in the eyes of Kanak Lata. She was now like a teacher, who had ultimately won.

Now there was no complaints, with Munna in hand, Mohan Babu followed her. Kanak Lata brought some water for him, before settling down wanted to tell his story, but Kanak Lata didn't listen to him, she said, "Take bath and change your clothes". The cloth were changed but grown up beared was still there, before sitting on the dining, Kanak Lata asked maid to take child out for some time, "No no", let him sit here and made him sit in front of his plate on table. Munna and Mohan Babu started feeding each other. He started telling him his story, "O son, I have been moving for a year from place to place to temple and ashrams. Wherever I went they took me as a new one and they didn't care for my habits. One sadhu asked me, go and bring water from the well. In another place, the head of the Mutt told me, you are a new one, and you don't know custom of the place, listen you have to stay in kitchen. After feeding everyone, you are allowed to take food. Then at night massage the legs of the head priest, Kanak Lata said, "Take your food! half an hour is gone". He grappled food and asked will I have some more Prasad, Kanak Lata fed him belly full. Now the story again started, Mohan Babu was not tired of telling stories. When his son and daughter in law found him in the house, they are very happy. Anil said, "I have taken leave for a week; tomorrow I am going to take mother to village, you will stay here". "Neither you nor your mother will go to the village, I will go and come back after making arrangements there, then I will stay here with you all but let me stay here for a few days and play with my grandson. The decision of her husband made everybody happy. Kanak Lata said, "As long as my health is good, I will go to the village, I have many things there, and how can I leave my friends there. I will come at the interval of every two or three months. Anil was overwhelmed with the practical knowledge of his mother and as far as Mohan Babu was concerned, now he will do whatever Kanak Lata, his wife will say. She didn't prevent him from remaining as a household sannyasi.

□

# 18

# At That Very Moment

For a week now, my mind was worried. Suddenly I thought of going to my father's house. Worry subsided somehow but no excuse came to my mind. How should I tell him, for twenty years I have been making excuses. Whenever I wanted to go to Chappra, it took a few days to convince him "what is the hurry to going to your father's house. Yesterday your father came and last week your mom visited you". This question was enough to silence the voice of the prompt wife. Really why I was in such a hurry, father used to visit me, once-twice or sometimes three times a week.

Sometimes, my mother has to consult some doctors or visit some cinema or circus. Sometimes the excuse was that she hasn't seen her daughter for a long time. Mother had to make so many excuses to my father. My father used to understand the silent eagerness of mother to see me and bring her to the town to meet me.

After my marriage for about two years, mother didn't come to our rented house. On every small and big festive occasion, she used to call me home, usually father used to take me. In the village, parents lived alone and my only brother's family was in Kolkata. They had to plead with the son-in-law, He said, "At present it is time for her studies and she is weak in English. "If she visits her parents house so frequently what will happen to her studies?" My father would take more care of my studies than my husband. But he used to plead, "What can I do, her mother doesn't agree and she stops eating and drinking, I will take her in the evening and send her back next morning. I will keep the rickshaw ready and early morning she will reach the town".

"Behind the curtain, I would like to read the brow of my husband. Before my father, he wouldn't be rude but inside he would murmur". This close distance of my in laws house at six miles is a headache.

I would request him to keep quiet so that father shouldn't hear him. But my week indications were answered in a strong voice," "Go Go have enough of sweet porridge. In the examination you will get a big zero". Ignoring his dissonance, I would quickly put my clothes in a bag and get ready to go with my father. With weak voice my father would say "Her mother has requested you (son-in-law) also to come". "No I will not go, I have to go for a meeting today". The answered was prepared as if the question was out.

"Yes you are correct, how can you have leisure, I always tell her but she is illiterate and she can't imagine the busy schedule of other people. But she is eager to feed stuffed *pudi and sweet* porridges. She wants her son-in-law and daughter also to come, how can I make her understand that in town, people keep eating varieties of sweets daily. What is in your stuffed pudi and sweet porridge?" The rickshaw puller would ring his bell, this gave me relief. May be he loses his patience and denies permission to go with my father.

When I reached home, I found my mother waiting for me at the door, hearing the sound of rickshaw she would call, "O Bhulani, bring the lantern. In the dim light of lantern, she on her *machia,* she would count the people alighting from the rickshaw. The moment I touched her feet, she questioned, and your husband didn't come. Without answering, I entered the house, she was angry with my father, "You didn't bring my son-in-law, with so much labour, I prepared sweet porridge. With great pain, I got milk. During these days of festival, milk is not easily available. And stuffed *pudi* were prepared with so much spices. I think you didn't plead him to come. Father would get angry and speak angrily, "Stop your nonsense, why didn't you go to bring him. Will he leave his work for your home made food, such a big officer?" He would take down his cap and sit down in his easy chair. The mother would with great difficulty lift her heavy gouty body. She would use this time in hearing the angry words of my father.

"You are correct, how can we illiterate people know his work schedule, I in the morning, I will send something for him". And saying this she enters the house. Amending her plan, father said, "Not with anybody, early morning Madhu has to return and you send whatever you have with her". Then why you called her for one night. "Maze bread, curd rice, rice bread, kari bari, local delicacies were planned but how could she will make all these items in such a short time". Whatever she could prepare, she would keep for breakfast and rest would think of giving her at next visit. Father was very particular, he decided to send me early morning to the town. Mother would get up early and pack delicacies for me. To feed her son-in-law, she would give elaborate instructions.

When I reached town, I tried to hide these small bundles from his hawk eyes. But I couldn't hide it, he would make me realise the reality of this, "Madhu just think, how much would be the value of all this, five to ten rupees, are these not available in the town, you collect these food stuff, what will the people of your village think and our neighbour also?"

I kept silent as if I have no tongue in my mouth. He was very correct. Most of the items I couldn't use but I used to carry them. I used to argue with mother, "Ma your moong dal and mustard and corrinder and red chilli, lemon, cucumber I don't need. After all compared to my income of big officer husband, this is like a penny for him. This much my servant throws out. My dining table became a symbol of national integrity.

Instead of upma, dosa coconut preparations, my husband would ask for *tisi* and local varieties, I couldn't stop my mother from sending these items. Time passed, my children grew up. My mother used to come to my house and bring many items with her.

But as usual these items used to give my husband a bad taste in his mouth. The family was increasing and with that the expenditure of the household also. The expenditure of kitchen increased with the large number of drivers, servant's maid and peons. With increase in income I did not worry for expenditure as my expenditure went on increasing, the items and weight of things brought by my mother started decreasing, in spite of his objections the coming of items didn't stop. The site of opening those small items used to give me unconscious happiness.

I started going to my mother's place in my own car, mother had grown old her movement had stopped. I used to visit her at least once in two months. It was difficult for me to find time to visit her. My husband used to permit me to visit her for her illness. Once when I went to Chappra. My brother with his family had come to see mother. I was sitting with Kiran, Manju and Mukul. After a long time the courtyard was agog with sounds of Phua. I was anxious to talk to my bhabhi, my mom was shouting, "Come here, for a moment sit with me. Soon will be time for you to go; O God my waist and legs are at pain".

I left the company of children and sat down with my mother. She didn't have much to say. In low voice she said, "Go to the southern room, in a pot there are some *moong*. Take some maize Navin likes popcorn. Pravin is found of sweet porridge, take some flavoured rice. O my legs I can't get up".

I kept staring at her; she caught hold of my wrist and used to try to move my dozens of bangles. She would caress my arms and she would move her hand on my stomach, you have lost your weight. Go take the things I have told you, "I couldn't say no. My aunt from neighboring house had come, my mom requested her to prepare bundles for me. I felt bad; I don't know what the fear that didn't allow me to refuse those presents. My brother came with me to town. My husband was sitting on the *verrandah* and the moment he saw a peon carrying bundles from car, he shouted, "throw them away. Whenever she goes to her mom house she brings, I have asked her not to bring such things to my house".

The moment I came to the drawing room I looked back and indicated him to keep quiet. Why should I keep quiet? I told you many times don't bring these bundles here. Making his voice normal, he said, "come-come, when did you come", he was now welcoming my brother. I breathed a sign of relief. I feared lest my brother listen to his loud voice. My brother heard him or not his behaviour didn't betray this, neither did I ask him. Why should I make myself sad by asking whose fault was this? Was it my mother, who was on death bed or my husband, I thought it was wise to keep quiet.

Within a year mom died and the first death anniversary my father also followed her. I gathered courage to ask my husband "should I go to chhapra", and with the same he saw cunning eyes. "Now what is there in Chhapra, your parents are no more there, will you go for house darshan?" The question was straight and true to the letter. His gesture and voice has changed the meaning without caring for his words, I pleaded as child "Let me go, now it is almost a year, my bhabhi has also come". With a good advice he spoke, "You see it is hot weather and there is no electricity in the village and you will go with children".

"I will leave the children here and come back tomorrow", the moment he agreed I got ready. He told his driver to take her to Chhapra and I will get my jeep from the office. With watching his liberal tenderness, I got courage to say, "I will stay for two days. I was going to my mom house exactly after a year as I visited on last ceremonies of my father. In the mean time, nobody came to call me, neither did I go there. My bhabhi had come to village to look after the sale of mangoes, litchis and store grains from the field. My neice, Kiran and her husband also have come, I was happy that I had permission to go. While going to Chhapra, my blood throbbed and I was tension free. Usually my husband would be irritated at the time of going and coming from the village. Now there was no probability of his anger on my return. Now that mom is no more who will arrange bundles, she used to create unnecessary headache. My mom had died after suffering great pain. The sorrow of her separation was mitigated by the thought that death has at least vanished the pain.

I reached the village, the car stopped at the gate of my brother. All the children of the neighbour came rushing, Madhu phua has come. My nephew and bhabhi also came out of the house. Everyone was happy at my sudden arrival. Suddenly, I felt that my blood vessel was numbed as if my legs were going behind. After crossing the stair cases, I found the easy chair, near the door was the *machia*. The whole atmosphere was the same, my bhabhi had not made any changes. Near the empty easy chair, suddenly my legs stopped and I forcefully prevented my hands from folding. Now I wanted to enter the room, on the empty machia of my mother as if she held my sari. I forcefully entered the room. Bhabhi had spread the cot in the yard, women and children surrounded us, from courtyard to the door, every place was full. After a long time, all have gathered together but at this atmosphere's emptiness was pursuing me. I realised my mom was staring at my every limb. I was disturbed. My aunt quickly perceived my condition and she said my daughter is remembering her dead mother, As if somebody pierced a needle in the wound. Kiran brought tea for me. Looking at my tears she said, "What has happened to phua? "Nothing" said my aunt. And with her apron, she wiped my tears. But her eyes were full of tears. She got up and went to wash her eyes. The people in the neighborhood were very surprised to find that as usual I didn't leave early morning. Aunt asked my bhabhi, "Is Madhu not going today?" The old parents were afraid of the son-in-law and used to send the daughter early in the morning to the town. My bhabhi spoke with confidence, "I am not afraid of her husband, she will go after two days. She has come after long gap and I don't know when she will come next time to the village". My cultured bhabhi, didn't leave anything in my hospitality. She used to prepare fish, mutton and pulaou in a new style. But my tongue was used to the old taste that used to bring tears to my eyes. It was difficult for me to hide the tears from the members of reception committee. At the time of departure two boxes of mangoes, litchis, jackfruits, sweets and hence the car was full. I requested my bhabhi not to put so many things she replied, "I have not purchased from the market and children will enjoy these. My aunty was very happy to see these thinghs. She thanked bhabhi and said, "You have done a good thing; this is the way to send sister-in-law. Her mother would put many small bundles; my bhabhi found that I was not there. She confided to my aunt, "Do you know, her husband once was angry for these small bundles before my husband". He said many harsh words to his mother. Your mother-in-law didn't take food for days and died after a month. My aunt wiped her eyes with her apron".

I have heard the talk from the next room, I was very much upset and tears trickled down my cheeks. I didn't want to show this to my bhabhi, She shouted from outside, "Kiran and Kilash will go with you, they also have to return". Suddenly she remembered something and said, "O kiran, bring some small piece of cloth and put some moong, maize flour and mustard". Handing over small piece of cloth she asked me Madhu Ji, whatever Kiran wants to give her from the southern rooms. In the meantime I set breakfast for you. Once again my tears started, with great effort I stopped them and then prepared big and small bundles. At the time of taking out bundles Kailash was angry, his face was red.

At the sound of the horn, my husband came out, I was looking at him and he was looking at the dickey of the car. The peon was taking out the boxes of the fruits and putting them on verandah, my husband was like a custom inspector deputed at Nepal-Bihar border. The driver after dropping the fruit boxes, started the car, the inspector was disappointed as if smuggling was stopped. But he stared looking minutely at the boxes of litchis and mangoes. With heavy heart I dragged my feet inside my house.

Navin came running and with pleasant surprise said, "Where has mummy come from with so many things". Pravin said, "Papa you said that mummy went to *nani's* house but why she has brought so many things. A sad custom inspector said in low voice, "Your mummy had gone to *nani's* house. Navin, pravin, parimal, servants and drivers took the boxes inside. My husband came in; I was standing before the window and looking at the empty sky. Coming behind me and patting my shoulders he said, "Madhu no mother lives forever, like a rain filled river, my eyes started flowing. And he also started crying. At that very moment he realised my Mom's absence.

□□□